D0914200

SLEEP HAS HIS HOUSE

Also available from Michael Kesend Publishing, Ltd.
By Anna Kavan

ASYLUM PIECE

SLEEP HAS HIS HOUSE

by

ANNA KAVAN

Michael Kesend Publishing, Ltd.

 Published in the United States by Michael Kesend Publishing, Ltd. 1025 Fifth Avenue, New York, N.Y. 10028. Originally published in Great Britain by Peter Owen Limited.

Library of Congress Cataloging in Publication Data
Edmonds, Helen Woods
Sleep has his house.
I. Title
PR6009.D63Z52 1980 823'.912 [B] 79-26730
ISBN 0-935576-00-2

Manufactured in the United States of America

. . . in a strange land, on the
borders of Chymerie . . . the god of
sleep has made his house . . . which of
the sun may naught have, so that no man
may know aright the point between the day
and night. . . . Round about there is growing on the
ground, poppy which is the seed of sleep . . . a
still water . . . runs upon the small stones
. . . which gives great appetite for
sleep. And thus full of delight
the god of sleep has his
house. JOHN GOWER

LIFE IS TENSION or the result of tension : without tension the creative impulse cannot exist. If human life be taken as the result of tension between the two polarities night and day, night, the negative pole, must share equal importance with the positive day. At night, under the influence of cosmic radiations quite different from those of the day, human affairs are apt to come to a crisis. At night most human beings die and are born.

Sleep has his house describes in the night-time language certain stages in the development of one individual human being. No interpretation is needed of this language we have all spoken in childhood and in our dreams ; but for the sake of unity a few words before every section indicate the corresponding events of the day.

SLEEP HAS HIS HOUSE

IT is not easy to describe my mother. Remote and starry, her sad stranger's grace did not concern the landscape of the day. Should I say that she *was* beautiful or that she did not love me? Have shadows beauty? Does the night love her child?

WHAT A FEARFUL thing it can be to wake suddenly in the deepest hours of the night. Blackness all round; everything formless; the dark pressing against the eyeballs; the darkness a black thumb pressed to the starting eyeballs distended with dread. At first I don't know what I am to become.. I am like an embryo prematurely expelled from the womb. I remember nothing, know nothing: I haven't the least idea what is making me tremble all over like a person suffering the effect of shock. It happens to be the cruellest shock of all I am suffering from: the brutal violence of the birth shock.

I must find myself, I cannot drown in so black a sea, and I begin to strike out, threshing about desperately, this way and that, in pursuit of the images which appear, transparent as the shadows of icicles, incorporated in the night-plasma. Floundering among the waves, my head just above water, the most shapeless water, I plunge into a picture: but at once the outlines disintegrate, coldly . . . coldly . . . no frost flower decorating a window-pane vanishes more inexorably in the sun. Into the ephemeral images I dive, one after the other: sometimes one crystallizes into a brief sharpness—never to permanence. At last I dive with extraordinary accuracy into my own body, which I see laid out, high and dry, above the receding tide. I am lying there like a long white fish on a slab. Is it a bed or a bier that I'm lying on? Or have I really been washed up on some beach or other?

I feel the sides of the thing I'm lying on with my hands. Yes, it's a bed, no doubt of that. I'm myself, alive on a bed, not drowned or exposed in a morgue. Nor am I a fish on a fishermonger's marble slab.

So far so good. But what bed it is that I'm lying on I'm not able to say. What room is this? I look round for a window. Is it there . . . ? Or there . . . ? Or perhaps over there, where, in any case, I feel a door ought to be? There's not a single gleam, not a glimmer, to give me a clue. The whole room is as black as pitch. In fact, I'm not at all sure that it is a room. Something suggests to me now that I'm on board ship; I might be floating adrift on some tranquil sea. And yet there's no sound, no motion, nothing to indicate either sea or land. Like a ghost train my life streams through my head, and I don't know which point of the compass I'm facing.

How dark it is. The moon must have stolen away secretly. The stars have thrown their spears down and departed. There seems to be nothing except primordial chaos outside the window. Utterly still, utterly alone, I watch the darkness flower into transient symbols. And now there is danger somewhere, a slow, padded beat, like cushioned paws softly approaching. What an ominous sound that is to hear in the night.

THE *first* place I remember was warm and sunny. I remember the flowers that grew there, and trees smelling of summer. The sun always seemed to shine in that country. I don't remember seeing my parents often. A Japanese houseboy looked after me most of the time. He was kind and told me many beautiful stories. He drew pictures to please me, plants and magical fishes.

UP, UP, up swings the little boat, gently, languidly climbing the enormous swell, like drifting thistledown, scarcely seeming to move. The tiny boat hardly seems to be moving at all, but up it climbs on the huge blue undulation, up, up, towards the solemn clouds standing in tall arcades, far too bright for the eyes. In a dazzle of utter blue, the boat climbs to the wave's shoulder. And down, down, down, it begins to travel, with emerald facets glittering on the blue. The descending swell burns translucent, a fiery barrow, entombing the amethyst shades of sea-lions, over which the little boat glides with blithe unconcern.

Painted ultramarine, with embossed eyes vigilant for water demons, the boat itself is the centre, the focal point, of a vast sea dream. And it is dreamlike and noticeable that the boat is oarless, sailless, motorless, moving apparently of its own volition and without any help from the yellow man who sits in the stern, smiling down at his drawing of colored inks. Held in fingers the color of old piano keys, his brush traces the lines which are finer than hairs. The smooth progress of the boat does not disturb the accuracy of his touch. Intent, with the sun glistening like a second reflected sun on his bowed head, he placidly continues to map out a spidery complex of strokes, paying no attention to the course on which he is being carried. And now the swells rear into monsters plunging thunderously to the shore; but the boat has passed the protecting reef and floats on the shallow water. Here through a sparkling window the sea-floor can be seen, coral citadels, battlemented with shells of peculiar shapes and colors, parks and thickets of weed and gardens of lacy crimson sea-fern. The inhabitants of these subaqueous regions pass under the boat serenely on their mysterious business. Some are beautiful creations, some grotesque, some delicate as spun glass, others clumsy like the outcome of a bungled experiment; some baleful, some amusing, some benign; some fearsome or weird in their exaggerated strangeness. They are equipped with every conceivable variation of color, texture and form: with frills, fans, fringes, spines, tentacles, filaments, helmets, swords; with appendages like trailing banners; with veils, periscopes, carapaces, suckers, pincers, razors, nets. This is clearly the source from which the yellow artist in the boat draws his inspiration. The picture is finished. He holds it up and smiles at the complicated fantasy evolved by his brush-strokes. He smiles, the smile growing unclear as a breaker shatters its glassy curve on the reef, and a miniature rainbow, a storm-dog, slowly dissolves in spray over his head.

The dream foreground which reappears is obscured by mantles of nostalgic melancholy. A soft antique rain falls. Twilight. The colors lavender to pigeon and pearl grey with the delicate green of a weeping willow tree on the left. Behind the willow hangs the suggestion of a cascade. In the middle distance, centrally placed, a small hill with a tomb—a simple shrine, it looks like—at the top.

The remote voices of antiquity whisper quietly together: the willow; the rain; the cascade. Presently a shadow moves on the lower slopes of the hill; at first a blur, gradually becoming distinguishable as the back view of a fox, belly close to the ground, long brush extended, cautiously stealing upwards. It moves along so secretly that it appears to creep like a snake. When it has almost reached the top, the fox stops, turns its head, and looks slowly from side to side. With its head turned, it crouches there for a while in furtive forlornness, then suddenly disappears. In its place stands a young girl with long and very lovely hair who clasps her grave-clothes with one hand, runs to the tomb and vanishes inside.

Immediately the light changes and brightens, the rain stops; there is a stir of suppressed excitement, an impression of movement, although no new shapes appear. The mists in the foreground weave and divide, expanding, convolving, coagulating, in the middle air where they remain suspended and faintly vibrant, transfused with rosy light which grows stronger and stronger as if the sun were rising behind them. As brightness culminates, the mist breaks into countless shimmering flakes, a swarm of petals speckles and flutters the air, a charming group of cherry trees is nodding gracefully in full flower.

Plangent music is heard as a crowd of courtiers

enters, escorted by attendants who at once retire unobtrusively into the background, while the ladies and gentlemen arrange themselves under the cherry trees as if for the opening movement of a ballet. These are people of brilliance and distinction; it is impossible to imagine anything more decorous than their behaviour, at once natural and ceremonial, or more elegant than their elaborate garments "in which, down sleeve and skirt, fold chimes with fold in every imaginable harmony of texture and hue". A sort of masque is now played out among them, with much gallantry on the part of the gentlemen and many exchanges of formal gifts, each with its appropriate message, sprays of blossom concealing love notes, caskets no less sparkling then the epigrams they contain. From time to time someone sings or plays on the lute or the zithern, or recites a poem fitting the situation of the moment. There is nothing in the least stilted about all this, and one gets the impression that it is not really a charade that is taking place, but a recognized ritual of conduct, the genuine expression of cordiality among these cultured and decorative exquisites.

Several moon-faced children are moving about here and there, and they are made a great fuss of, caressed and petted by everybody. The whole party is continuously in a state of fluidity, groups forming and breaking and re-forming with different units, so that the effect is that of a dazzling and constantly changing color design, like those boxes of colored beads which can be shaken into innumerable shining patterns. Two figures only remain static, the hub around which all this brilliance revolves. Perhaps it is Prince Genji himself with long hanging sleeves, the bright scarlet of his under-robe showing through the flowery tissue of his mantle, who is smiling so enigmatically at the First Princess in her clove-dyed silk dress.

Gradually the picture starts to fade out. Light, which has all the time emanated from some point behind the cherry trees, for several minutes has been imperceptibly fading and is now no longer rosy; the blossom-cloud has lost its lamplike glow and is mere pale flowering cherry. There is a general lowering of tone and tempo so that the figures of the courtiers seem less alive, their clothing less gay, their voices less melodious, as they slowly disperse. The music lingers a little while after the last one has vanished; but the notes diminish and dwindle into the tinkling of a child's musical-box.

Silence. Livid swaths of light fall as if cut by a scythe. The trunks of the trees are obliterated, but the blossom can still be seen, a compressed blizzard, pallidly churning and milling. The unobserved and forgotten guards in the distance now suddenly assume drastic importance as they begin to converge on the center. They wear bulky dark clothes and their faces are obscured as by masks or helmets. Each is an incipient catastrophe, intensely ominous in his stiff hierarchic motions.

A loudening rush of noise like escaping steam hisses out of the spinning mass in mid-air and seems to draw the figures together. As they finally gather in a compact group under this pallid magnet, they are caught in a funnel of dead lead-grey light flaring down from it, and for the first time are to be seen in detail. They are small, dressed in some indeterminate uniform, their faces under their helmets formally, flatly, impersonally evil. They are looking straight ahead, as if posed for a picture. Their expressions set, childish and racially inaccessible. After a while darkness steadily and methodically plucks them out of sight one by one.

The ashy remnant of what was once cherry blossom continues to rain through the blackness while the accompanying noise expands, spouts and crackles into an ear-splitting engine-roar. As this shattering thunder becomes quite unbearable, it explodes into silence. At the same instant the whirling formlessness bursts into a shower of leaflets which are catapulted in all directions. They drift downwards, and there is a momentary glimpse of them sucked and eddying madly in the up-draught of a flaming jungle village, fired palm trees ablaze and streaming. Vacuum.

LATER we crossed the sea to a colder country where my mother was bored and sad. We lived in a house full of things kept brightly polished. Visitors admired the house and everything in it. Most of all they admired my mother. She was like a queen in the house—a princess in exile. All the shine of the house was quenched by my mother's sadness. It was not a gay house in spite of the bright things in it. No, the house was not really gay at all.

THE DREAM scene comes to light as a comprehensive view of a garden suburb seen from the air. The whole layout is visible. At one extremity the conglomeration of city outskirts: slums, factories, converging tram, train, bus routes, arterial roads. At the other end the opening countryside: fields, scattered industrial areas, a golf course, a few hills and small woods. Then a closer view of the suburb. It's a high-class residential district. The streets are wide and planted with trees, the geometrical rows of houses stand in neat gardens, there is a busy shopping center, solid neo-Georgian municipal buildings, a crescent of fake Tudor houses in herringbone brick disguises, business premises. It's summer. A windy and sunny day. All the gardens are spick-and-span with orderly flower-beds and lawns carefully mown. A few have tennis courts; others have pools, rockeries, sundials, effigies of rabbits, toadstools or gnomes. Some, not many, tradesmen's vans and shiny private cars sliding along the roads. A bus draws itself smoothly past the public gardens. Smoke rises in fat curlicues from prosperous chimneys. More insistent than anything, dwarfing the whole scene to papier-mâché cuteness, the enormous blue undisciplined sky with robustious clouds bucketing across.

A straight view of one of the widest streets from ground-level follows.

A dark limousine, an eight-year-old model, but beautifully kept, is being driven along this street by a chauffeur in hogskin gloves. A white gate with THE ELMS painted on the top bar. Appropriate elm trees at each side. The gate is hooked open. The car makes a careful curve and drives in. A glimpse of lawn; cutting the edge of the grass with long-handled shears, a gardener, who glances up with skimming non-interest. The front door comes into prominence with porch and flanking hydrangeas in pots. The car stops; chauffeur gets out of his seat, rings the door bell, comes back and opens the door of the car from which emerges a lady of no particular age, dressed for paying a call. Her dress and hat are expensive, very much toned-down versions of the season's fashionable styles. A maid in white afternoon apron and cap opens the house door for her.

All these people, the lady, the chauffeur, the gardener, the maid, have the same face which they wear as if it were a mask, indifferent, decorous, non-descript, and quietly, negatively repressive. If the chauffeur and his employer were to change clothes no one would notice the difference.

Meanwhile, a door opens into the usual drawing-room, arranged with half-taste, too many knick-knacks, too many vases of flowers. The casement windows have chintz curtains and the same material has been used for covering the sofa and chairs. The room only differs from other suburban drawing-rooms because a good deal of the bric-à-brac comes from the East.

The visitor sits down with her feet close together. She has been in the room before. As she takes off her gloves and smooths the creases out of them, she glances about the room, stamping it with the tepid pass of her recognition.

After a minute the door opens and the mistress of the house—for the sake of economy she may as well be called A—comes in. She is nearing forty, her still young face is attractive in spite of the discontent harassing it. During a rather long-drawn-out pause she stands in the doorway at the far end of the room. There is plenty of time to observe her. The details of her appearance become clearly defined; narrow neurotic face under bright curled hair, uneasy hands, plain light dress very simple compared with the visitor's outfit. This woman's restless, artistic personality is considerably over-emphasized by contrast with the mediocre, phlegmatic mask-face worn by all the others. However, she seems a little too dramatic to be quite convincing. There is a suggestion of planned exhibitionism about her pose in the doorway which is so prolonged as to produce an effect of tension. As she at last shuts the door quietly and comes forward, in dream fashion the room gradually heightens and elongates: at the same time an invisible sponge passes over it, eliminating detail; windows are blotted out one after another till only a single tall window remains, admitting a flat neutral light, between stiff fluted curtains: so that she advances into a long, cold, lofty, uncolored room which is empty except for the unaltered chintz chair where the visitor sits and one or two other indistinct objects which symbolize furniture.

With each step A takes, a modification, corresponding to what's happening in the room, progresses in her own appearance. All her tragic potentialities are brought out and accentuated. She grows taller and thinner, her face chalk-white and haggard, her hair curls into a stiff sacrificial crown. Even her dress changes color, turning red-black, so that she eventually stands like a dark pillar in front of the blank window. She has her back to the room and to the visitor who has remained sitting in the flowery armchair, feet side by side, smoothing the creases out of her folded gloves.

How you must miss it all, the visitor says.

Synchronizing with her perfectly commonplace voice, the light starts to grow dim, diminishing steadily until the room becomes quite dark except for the luminous window against the lower part of which, in the exact center, A's sombre silhouette remains standing throughout, absolutely motionless.

How you must miss it all, the visitor says.

The romance of the East, a precisely similar voice says, answering, in precisely the same ladylike, banal, superficial tone. From different parts of the room other identical voices eject similar comments: The color, The mystery, The gay social life, and so on. As each voice speaks, a pasty finger of light rambles towards it, just barely indicating repetitive replicas of the original caller and establishing the existence of a chorus distributed round the dark room.

Every time the light touches a new speaker she is shown sitting with consciously crossed ankles, consciously ladylike, her face tilted to vacancy, smiling the conventional vapid smile of the afternoon visitor.

While this goes on, the view outside the window, materializing from nothing, presents a sequence of Far-Eastern scenes dissolving into one another, tremendously fast, immensely disorganized. It is never possible to grasp these visions completely (they are partly hidden by the black shape standing with her back to the room) because of their speed and the confused way in which they evolve themselves at all angles and on different size scales.

For instance: a minuscule landscape with palms and temples, instantly smothered by the overflowing of a gigantic yellow river in spate; slither of water yeastily regurgitating refuse and half-seen domestic objects; rafts on which families are living, fishing, washing, cooking, sleeping, engaging in intimate occupations of all descriptions, suddenly soar upwards like magic carpets: a tangle of upside-down horses' legs racing; intersecting arcs of swung polo-sticks swooping: ambiguous smiling bland oriental faces: gathering of Very Important People (white, most of them, but a sprinkling of highly decorated and jewelled nabobs in magnificent costumes for picturesque local color); personages with orders; uniforms; elaborately dressed women. Then, getting more tangled and chaotic, a crazy avalanche of flowers, mosquito nets, champagne bottles, electric fans: hands carrying trays, golf bags, rackets, wraps; guns, whips; white hands, brown hands, yellow hands;

hands lighting cigarettes, cigars; holding weapons, holding glasses, holding reins, rackets, bats, sticks, clubs; holding other hands: mouths with lipstick, with moustaches, with thick lips, with thin lips; Eastern mouths, Western mouths; mouths shouting orders, kissing, singing, drinking, whispering: liners, trains, cars, tongas, traps; baggage, horses, mules, bullocks, sampans, rickshaws; children, dogs, coolies, ayahs: ships sailing, troops marching, storms breaking, doors opening, moons rising, suns setting, trees blowing; dust-storms, thunderstorms; meetings, intrigues, assignations, partings.

Immediately after this the somewhat more stabilized formality of a black tree-trunk, of which A's body forms a part, with perfectly naked bilateral boughs, immediately sprouting several huge white trumpet-shaped flowers.

There is an infinitesimal break in continuity as the dream angle changes a little. The comments of the chorus veer, but scarcely, and continue

you must find it a great change living here
very different indeed
perhaps a trifle dull after all your travels
although we have our own interests too
there's always plenty going on in a quiet way
the bridge parties
the tap dancing at the health class
the sale of work
the Women's Institute meetings
the garden fête at the vicarage
dinner at Dr. Moore's (such a charming man).

The accompanying pictures outside the window by

contrast with the previous sequence are very slow and definitive; their materialization is painstakingly realistic and they follow the spoken phrases meticulously, with strict, but not exaggerated, attention to rigorous suburban respectability, dullness.

And then it's so easy to run up to town for a theatre or a film.

Quick in the vision the closed car sliding along, a man with a white silk scarf at the wheel, a woman beside him wearing an evening wrap of some kind; their dummy figures sitting stiffly erect, their white faces calcified in boredom. Branching out of the car fading, the black arterial road with lateral streets swings back to the black tree, the black woman's body clamped to the tree. This time the flower-spurting is reversed, the petal wreckage dripping down flaccid, a slimy tatter of dissolution, semi-liquid decay.

The light goes back sharply to normal, returning to the dream the suburban drawing-room, the chintzes, the knick-knacks, the vases of flowers. A has just sat down on the sofa. Under polite composure her limp attitude protests against hard reality. The visitor, sitting exactly as she has sat from the start, is saying something indistinguishable to her as the maid comes in at the door pushing a trolley with bright crested silver tea-service, plates of thin bread-and-butter, absurdly small cucumber sandwiches, macaroons.

A little girl with fair hair—she is unmistakably the child of her mother and so could be called B—peeps in through the open door, unnoticed by the grown-ups; then tiptoes away.

OUR house always seemed especially quiet, as if people spoke there only in lowered voices. My parents seldom had time for talking to me. No one talked to me much: but the rain often used to whisper. It rained a lot and the rain kept whispering to me. In the long afternoons when the rain filled each window and shadows met together in every corner, I sometimes thought of the sun and the Japanese houseboy. It was lonely in those rooms dark with my mother's sadness and with the rain on the windows. The rain shut off the house by itself in a lonely spell.

In time I found out what it was that the rain whispered. I learnt from the rain how to work the magic and then I stopped feeling lonely. I learnt to know the house in the night way of mice and spiders. I learnt to read the geography of the house bones. Invisible and unheard I scampered down secret tunnels beneath the floor boards and walked a tight-rope webbing among the beams.

After that I never wished for children to play with, or for the Japanese houseboy to tell me fantastic stories. Hidden by curtains, sheltered in cupboards, ambushed in foxholes between the tables and chairs, I transmuted flat daylight into my night-time magic and privately made for myself a world out of spells and whispers.

THE PRE-REALIST fantasia opens up in an inchoate sort of Marie Laurençin dream of delicate tints. No form to speak of. Just a pearly billowing and subsiding of fondant chromatics; baby blue, candy pink, lemon-icing yellow, all sweetly harmonious and insipid like a débutante's bon-bon box tied up in cellophane and big satin bows. After a sufficiency of this things begin to take shape, but as we are taking a long view of the time-stream and creation hasn't occurred yet, there's naturally a lot of fluidity. A tinkling twinkling musical-box tune, with accompanying Tyrolean or Swiss dancers, fancy peasants, rose-wreathed cupids, angels with night-gowns and cheeks like pomegranates, is liable to translate any minute into a Brahms symphony and the austere discipline of the *ancien corps de ballet*.

In the same way the mountain which presently arches itself up like a cat's back is perhaps Mount Olympus, or perhaps Mount Sinai, or perhaps it is a cat's back and not a mountain at all. Assuming that it's a mountain, as a closer view seems to confirm, one gets an impression of pellucidity more appropriate to a mirage. There are crystalline snow slopes, diaphanous groves of trees, hyaline rocks, and, in the immediate foreground, a small lake, clear as glass, the translucent waters of which have surely never been contaminated by so much as a minnow.

Perhaps it is an extreme northern latitude that gives such rarefied transparency to the scene, lighted, as it appears to be, by the limpid coruscations of the aurora borealis. And this is a theory which gains a certain amount of support from the arrival of a party of hikers, of a truly Scandinavian robust comeliness, who proceed to picnic by the water's edge. Every one of these picnickers, old as well as young (for there are several elderly people among them), is remarkable for his or her splendid physique, and for a skin tanned to a glorious golden brown. As might be expected of such magnificently fit specimens, they are full of abounding gusto and energy. Every now and then members of the group, unable to contain their *joie-de-vivre*, go off to run races or engage in contests of strength, calling aloud to each other by oddly familiar names. A good deal of indiscriminate necking, of a specially exuberant, whole-hearted and unself-conscious variety, also goes on; and this gives rise to sudden jealousies, apt to culminate in violence or in malicious pranks and practical jokes. It is noticeable that these childishly evanescent loves and quarrels spring up and are forgotten with equal ease; and perhaps this has something to do with the wine with which all the haversacks seem to be well supplied.

The irresponsible holiday atmosphere has a good innings before certainly pronouncedly killjoy clouds, gathering censoriously over the lake, begin to deluge the picnickers with torrential rain. It's no ordinary mountain storm that comes on, but an absolute cloud burst, a cataclysmic jet of watery disapproval, a purge which attacks the gay party with dank tenacity, never letting up until it has succeeded in washing them out of the picture entirely.

And now that the clouds clear away the whole aspect of the mountain has changed. Vanished the lake, the roseate dream-light, the ethereal snows. Instead, a prosaic materialism illuminates a dado of arid crags behind a laboratory where a scientist is working, an old fellow with a grubby grey beard reminiscent of those superannuated physicians who dodder out their last days at obscure Continental spas. He is wearing a voluminous white overall tied with strings at the back, and this gives him a grotesque likeness to a stout elderly *bonne*. The overall, beneath which his broad-toed black boots poke out like obstinate tortoises, is none too clean, being spotted, not only with spilled food and gravy, but by traces of the various experiments with which he is grumpily occupied. Back and forth he lumbers between his microscope and his reports, frequently pausing to consult a huge reference book, so massive that it might almost be made of stone, but without ever seeming to find the formula that he wants. A specially baffling point teases him, he paws at the great tome, shakily turning the pages with his vein-knotted hands.

He doesn't see the face watching him through the window, the cretinous grin under the shapeless straw hat full of holes. The village idiot peeps in round the post of the open door, grows bold seeing the old man so absorbed, and cautiously tiptoes into the room. The idiot boy advances in shambling stealth a little nearer the table where something is spluttering over a burner; cunningly keeps his eye on the reader; jerks himself nearer still. He is attracted by the bubbling mess in the tube; then fascinated by it; his hand stretches slyly towards it, draws back, fumbles to it again; he twitches in violent excitement, grimacing at it; clutches it.

The whole bag of tricks flashes up at his touch in an explosion of glittering dust. There's a split second's glimpse of the vast sad blackness of infinity before the perfectly bare void is spattered by this glittering exsurgence, this bursting fountain of molecules, instantly crystallizing to sequins of differing size. And now at once begins the fiery development of comets, suns, planets, nebulæ; constellations are clotted together; worlds rush forth on their immense navigations; the monstrous efflorescence of the universe burgeons in the flick of an eyelash. Creation is under way. The solar system is off. Larger and more brilliant blaze the globes, the stars roar past like stratoliners to destinations not checked in quadrillions. The billiard-ball earth swings up and flattens colossally underfoot. The thunderous revving of the cosmic machines settles to the steady beat of eternity.

Right in the middle of all this, in a quiet place, the little girl B sits reading a book. She is sitting on short fresh green grass, leaning against a tree, where it is quiet and cool. Everything here is springlike and very much simplified; just the grass and the innocent green tree and the child. Before long several other children appear and begin to play with red and green bean bags. They stand in two rows and each child throws the bag over his shoulder to be caught and passed on by the child behind. Their conduct is orderly, ritualistic, almost obsessional. They are completely concentrated on their serious attention to the rules of the game, their occasional subdued exclamations barely disturb the hush. Under the tree, B puts down her book and looks on. It's clear that she would like to join in, but she feels shy and needs some encouragement. The others pay no attention to her, they are quite absorbed in their game. At last B gets up and goes towards them. Play stops for a moment. A boy with a polite blank public-school face steps out and gravely invites her into the game.

Perhaps B is nervous, perhaps she doesn't understand the rules, perhaps she just means to introduce an innovation. Anyway, when it comes to her turn, she throws the red bean bag forward instead of back. The game breaks up at once, as if by telepathic agreement. The faces of the other children grow astonished and hostile. The polite boy in particular wears an outraged expression as he marshalls his companions away.

Left alone, B stands bewildered, looking in the direction where the players have vanished. After a moment, quickly and hopefully, her eyes are drawn to a man (it's her father, as a matter of fact) who walks along fast, dressed in dark town clothes and carrying a dispatch case and an umbrella. Her face turns upwards in expectation. But he is in too much of a hurry to notice her, he has important things on his mind, he passes on and scurries into an enormous office building which at this moment snaps up like an opera hat out of the ground to the right of the tree. As soon as he's in, the ornate double doors close behind him; but still, through the wrought-iron scrolls, he can be seen diminishing down room after room full of clerks, typists, desks, telephones, green-shaded lamps; door after transparent door shutting behind his back, till he is at last inaccessibly entombed as if in the heart of a gigantic formicary.

B, who has taken a few steps towards the building as if she meant to follow him, drifts back to the tree, on the other side of which a plain stone wall with a door in the center has now erected itself. From some distance off, A approaches aloofly, her hand already outstretched to the door. On this narrow door, with her left hand, with a blue-flashing ring, she raps in a deliberate fashion. While she is waiting for the door to open she turns her eyes slowly upon the child, at whom she looks directly and pensively. Then her eyes move, sliding without eagerness to the door which, opening, displays a dark space where it is just possible to distinguish the sculptured pallor of urns in the deep shadow. A goes inside. With two final, distinct clicks, the door is shut and locked. The little girl watches with the acceptance of perfectly uncomprehending fatalism, then sits down in her original place at the foot of the tree. As she picks up her book and starts reading, the wall and the office building dissolve unobtrusively, restoring the dream picture as it was to begin with. The only difference being that its vernal simplicity now holds a definite suggestion of loneliness, isolation.

WHEN my mother died I knew why the house had always been quiet. The house had been waiting and watching from the beginning, listening to the steps my mother danced with her death.

My father never told me about what had happened. No one said anything to me about the death of my mother and I never asked anyone. It was a question which could not possibly ever be asked. But I often wondered. At night, especially, I used to wonder. Sometimes I got afraid in the night, wondering about death and myself and my mother, and wishing that I could ask someone. But of course I knew I would never be able to ask such a question. My mother's death was the one thing I would never be able to speak of to anyone, no matter how frightened I was. That was the last thing I would ever do.

DAY TIME. Night time. Night the dark time: the time for wonder; the time for the question in daylight not to be spoken.

The question starts under the chest of drawers. At first it's impossible to be sure; there's still the chance that it may be something else. Perhaps a moth is attacking the thick winter sweater that's kept in the bottom drawer. The tough coarse ropes of wool are almost too much for him, but he won't give in, he won't admit that it's one too many for him, he tussles on in really heroic style, not taking abrasions and setbacks into any account at all. Or perhaps a beetle is boring into the wood. The bottom drawer sticks, it has to be pulled quite hard before it will open, and after a specially sharp tug a sprinkle of powdery shavings falls from the soft wood. A worm or a beetle could certainly dig himself in very cosily there; and without having to work unduly hard either.

However, it is not a moth in the bottom drawer, it isn't a beetle, it isn't the floor-boards stretching themselves in the dark. It's the question moving under the chest of drawers. It moves a little way on its belly, then craftily keeps still for a while like a tiger waiting to spring. Like a tiger the question crouches under the chest of drawers; a tiny tiger about the size of a mouse, and its striped coat black as velvet instead of tawny. Now it's moving again, flattened against the floor. Out in the room it crouches, expanding, accumulating its force. Soon it will be ready to pounce; its muscles bunch and ripple fearfully inside its skin. Larger and larger it grows: easily, beautifully, the tautened muscles levitate, launch the dark body into the air. The awful, lovely, stylized bow of the spring; effortless, almost languid, inevitable.

Where? Not the bright upstairs room that the morning shines through?

Mirror bevels, catching the sunlight, spit prisms so brilliant they seem cut out of rainbow diamonds. Held in a medallion of net-filtered sun, a white tallboy with elaborate mouldings; ornate, capacious and expensively Edwardian. Drawers glide silently in and out with glimpses of rolled stockings, gloves, blouses, underwear. The garments are lacy or hand-embroidered, there are scent sachets and lavender bags in the corners of the drawers. A travelling clock in its open morocco case chimes a light silver sound. Fluted silver candlesticks, crested, at the mantelpiece ends: the candles in them are pink. Monogrammed silver brushes and boxes yield smothered prismatic gleams. They are laid out on a wide white dressing-table in the bay window. The dressing-table matches the tallboy, the drawer fronts and the frame of the oval mirror criss-crossed with moulded ribbons and wreaths, the table-top, under its glittery paraphernalia, covered by a runner embroidered with pink roses. A similar flowered cloth on the table beside the bed, with a vase of carnations, bottle of Eno's fruit salts, harmless pillbox and water carafe arranged on a silver tray, all very clear in the sun. The net-curtained light coming through the window is candidly and peaceably laid over the pale, shiny, smooth satin bedspread. The sunlit effect is not sharp and not harsh, but insistent enough to give a frank innocuousness, openness, to everything in the room.

The door shuts on this and opens again, slowly, under the same ringed hand which we have seen already. A enters the same room; the only change is that now the sun is setting. Red sunset light fills the room so that it seems to be floating inside a druggist's beaker of colored water. Red in this sunset danger-light, her head held back tensely, the neck muscles tensing, the fragile exposed curve of the vulnerable white neck, taut, a vulnerable flower-stalk in the red room. With quick red springing wide and away from the neck, a vaporous darkening within the room, the silver suddenly blackened, the window rusted. The left hand leaps to the throat, convulsing, and flashing its dulled ring. Red sprays and stipples the bedspread with the delicacy of fine rain. Red cascades mistily from the open drawers of the tallboy, gingerly spreading fanwise over the whole floor, creeping towards the door

which opens and closes softly and carefully under A's hand as she goes out.

She closes the door with abstracted and almost tender attention, walking slowly away. It's a narrow gallery that she steps out into, a gallery running round three sides of a hall. Everything is very dark, the only light comes from an antique lantern down in the body of the hall which grudgingly emits a dusty glimmer through its horn windows. The gallery is in deepest shade. The panelling, the row of shut doors, are really nothing but guess-work. The hall roof is as high as a church, it wouldn't be out of place to see bats flitting about, or an owl roosting up on one of the rafters. The main part of the hall, down where the light is, presents a queer conflict between the florid and the austere. The bare lofty walls, the grim perspectives of shadow, the uncurtained and ecclesiastically shaped windows, have a severe monastic look. But this asceticism doesn't agree at all with the arsenic-green carpet, or with the sumptuous thronelike chair, glowing with scarlet silk under the lantern. The two colors, the arsenical carpet, the scarlet chair, the only visible colors, burn with the suppressed, dangerous intensity, the theatrical violence, with which occasional colors are over-emphasized in the usually neutral-tinted dream scene. There is a chemical suggestion about these tints, reminiscent of fires examined through smoked glass. One feels that they are too strong to be faced without some sort of screen.

A man is sitting in the chair, closely occupied with papers which he can barely see to read. Papers are stacked on a small table beside him: papers are in his hands, on his knees. Because of the position in which he is sitting, bent over his work, it's quite impossible to distinguish clearly anything about him. (But it's a pretty safe bet that he's the man who on a previous dream occasion was too busy to notice that his daughter wanted to ask him for his support.)

The general effect produced by all this is sinister and at the same time slightly phony. What really introduces the sinister element is that the dramatic trappings are somehow unconvincing. The massive walls might quite possibly be made of paper, the whole place might taper off into a flimsy tangle of wires and screens just out of eyeshot. And yet nothing positively suggests this. It's simply the ominous dream-feeling that appearances may suddenly slip out of themselves into something entirely different.

Visual reality might here be only a mask held in front of the face of some much more frightening reality in another dimension.

And this applies too in some way to A who, wrapped in a long dark garment, slowly starts to walk down the stairs. She is aware of the man sitting near the lamp without being disturbed by his presence. She walks quietly, but without making any special effort to avoid his notice; anyway, he is too far off to hear her. He is much farther away than he could possibly be. Glancing at him, her face is depersonalized, the face of someone seen in a photograph. When she gets to the foot of the stairs, coming into the lamp's radius, the shadows of the bannisters fall on her in successively widening strokes, like the flails of a threshing machine. At the foot of the stairs she stands still. She now has to embark on the arsenic sea, incandescent with mineral fires. It's a hard step for her to take. (Why are these endings called acts of weakness?) She stands on the last stair, her hand on the carved newel-post.

She puts one foot in front of her. As her foot

touches the carpet, the newel-post, very abnormally tall and massive, rears up behind her like a black tree. In an instantaneous flash-back of association comes the vaguely disturbing sensation of *déjà-vue*—— Has this happened already . . . where . . . ?

A takes a step forward; then another. She goes on to a door at the left of the lantern: that it is an outer door is shown by its numerous heavy fastenings; but the bolts are not bolted, the iron chain is hanging unhooked.

(*For a fractional moment, far off in the sea of universal identity, the slave, broken by torture, gravely and quietly speaking his antique wisdom:* Is there smoke in the room? If only a little I will remain; but if it is a very great smoke I will go out. For that door is always open. *Slow smoke rising solemn and funnel-shaped, as from a censer, conceals him, drifts him away.*)

A has only to turn the handle in order to go out. As she proceeds to do this, there is a perceptible increase in tension. She is set on holding herself aloof and dedicated to her purpose. She seems now definitely not to wish to attract the notice of the man sitting near. Nevertheless, there is a moment, just before she turns the handle, when something forces her to look at him, she even seems to make an unspoken appeal, though cynically without hope, as if to the indifferent and insensitive masses who understand nothing, see nothing. He, not absolutely unconscious, shuffles his documents, moves his feet on the carpet, roughening the bright pile. As tension accumulates, he looks up with a reluctant, resentful, only incipiently-aware expression. Does he hear something unusual? Is it raining outside? Has the wind got up suddenly? He doesn't see A. He would have to turn his head right over his shoulder to get her into his field of vision. For a few seconds he is restless, more irritated by the interference with his concentration than anything else. Soon he brushes the whole intangible interruption aside and goes on reading.

A slowly turns the door handle. And this door too she shuts very carefully and quietly behind her as she goes out into the garden of THE ELMS, where the gardener is cutting the edge of the grass with a pair of long-handled shears. She stands on the lawn quite close to him, watching the snipped grass blades fall on the gravel. She has the air of wishing to know with some part of her attention just how the shears are manipulated: but from this fractional escape her real ego stands always dissociated. The gardener does not look up. He wears an old soft-brimmed straw hat, his back is stiff, his head bent, the snicking rhythm of the shears does not hesitate.

While he stolidly goes on clipping, a car pulls up in front of the porch, the chauffeur gets out and rings the bell, the suburban lady steps down from the car, the maid comes to open the door of the house. These four people, the visitor, the gardener, the chauffeur, the maid, each wearing a similar mask-face under straw hat, hat with bird in it, peaked cap, muslin cap, are grouped together a few yards from A. The tableau holds in suspense while all the masks slowly swing towards A and remain fixed. Fright starting to appear on her face, A looks from one to the other, turns round, hurries away. As she goes out of the gate, the branches of the elms at each side reach out fumbling at her, their long arms fingered with groping leaves. A leaf falls: she begins running; others fall. Magnified, not in size but in prominence, dead leaves eddy to-and-fro on the ground, cluster in dusty drifts, scamper singly away.

And against a lead sky the bare tree-tops are laboring.

Are you afraid of the tigers? Do you hear them padding all round you on their fierce fine velvet feet?

The speed of the growth of tigers in the nightland is a thing which ought to be investigated some time by the competent authority. You start off with one, about the size of a mouse, and before you know where you are he's twice the size of the Sumatra tiger which defeats all comers in that hemisphere. And then, before you can say Knife (not a very tactful thing to say in the circumstances anyhow), all his boy and girl friends are gathered round, your respectable quiet decorous docile night turns itself into a regular tiger-garden. Wherever you look, the whole night is full of tigers leaping and loping and grooming their whiskers and having a wonderful time at your expense. There isn't a thing you can do about it apparently.

The wilder the tricks of the tigers, the more abandoned their games and gambols, the more diversely dreadful become the dooms of the unfortunate A in this dream. Her fugitive shape, black-swathed, vanishes at the end of every cul-de-sac. Through the cities of the world she pursues her fate, in streets where the dead eyes of strangers are no colder than the up-swarming lights which have usurped the brilliance of the stars. From shrouded platforms among the clouds she hurtles down. She plunges from towers strict and terrible in their stark fragile strength, delicate as jerboa's bones on the sky, perdurable with granite and steel. Slumped on his stained bar, Pete the Greek, beneath flyblown Christmas festoons which no one will ever remove, hears the screaming skid of wheels spouting slush with her blood. Limp as an old coat not worth a hanger, she is to be found behind numbered doors in hotel bedrooms; or dangling from the trees of country churchyards where leaning tombstones like feeble-minded ghosts mop and mow in the long summer grass. The weeds of lonely rivers bind her with clammy skeins; the tides of tropical oceans suck off her shoes; crabs scuttle over her eye sockets. Sheeted and anonymous on rubbered wheels she traverses the interminable bleakness of chloroform-loaded corridors. The sardonic yap of the revolver can be taken as the full stop arbitrarily concluding each ambiguous sentence.

An erratic but steadfast seeking, saraband and stalking of death by violence through the indifferent world. The dance enters upon a movement of weariness, desperation, finale. Just what its form, gesture and detail being variable and in no way permanent. For the occasion may be supposed a town house of a particular type, in an unfashionable, cheap district, a lodging-house possibly. There will be the area, spearheaded railings, crammed dustbins vomiting refuse; the street air stale in the unsweet warm evening; grimy, strident-voiced children, tired and cantankerous, quarrelling at their play. The house door, in need of painting, shabbily formal like a neglected and desecrated altar beneath the fanlight carrying the street number; perhaps a small bed-and-breakfast sign at one side. Inside, the hall, narrow, in gloom, worn linoleum double-tracked towards stairs and basement; a smell here of unappetizing meals, cabbage water and of the mackintosh hooked to the hatrack. A glazed pottery drainpipe, painted with bulrushes, used as umbrella-stand.

The staircase plods upwards, flagging at every flight, the creaking treads sustained by dirt-colored felt, trampled threadbare. At the top the back bedroom, dismal with furniture discards from many rooms; cluttered with glasses, cups, empty whisky and gin bottles; syringes, scattered tablets, powders spilled from their crumpled papers, needles, empty tubes labelled diamorph., etc., litter the floor. At the sash window, the dingy scum-white lace with the entangled light strangling meanly in it: on the brass bedstead, huddled bedclothes in disorder, beneath which the stiff, frightening shape of some human form can barely, inexorably, be discerned. A wicked black frieze of cowls and chimney-pots beyond the lightly air-sucked curtain, jagged angles of roofs and gables iron-sharp on the sky. The vacant, exhausted sky, like an old shell.

MY mother's death made no difference to the house except that she herself was no longer in it. At least her outward presence had gone away. Her sadness and her boredom stayed in the quiet rooms where I lived alone with shadows. As if they felt lonely, these two ghosts attached themselves to me and entered my night-time world. Sometimes I thought they had taken me for my mother, and I felt nearer to her through their nearness. Sometimes it seemed as if her departure had brought her too near. Sometimes her nearness was like a hand on my shoulder; then I felt frightened, and ran and jumped and turned somersaults even, trying to shake off her hand. But the hand always stayed on my shoulder as long as it wished to.

Sometimes, looking out of an upstairs window, I could feel my mother looking out of my eyes. Like people who from a bridge watch fish swimming below them, we saw the outside world as an alien element where we could take no part. Isolated behind the glass of our lonely window we looked down on the daily life which was not for us.

SHOUTING AND SINGING and hullooing his satellites the gregarious sun comes ranting upon the collective stage. After so many billion repetitions you might expect him to be getting the least bit perfunctory: but not he; no sirree. Like a conscientious actor determined to give the public full value for money, he rampages through his performance as enthusiastically as the first time he put on the act. Of course the rest of the cast plays up to him. The clouds jump to their opening positions, hurriedly snatching the gaudy properties of the co-operative scarf dance. On earth ocean bellows to ocean across the continents like allied commanders exchanging a salute of guns. The mutual greetings of the archipelagoes are more *intime*.

As the sunwaves break over the roof of the jungle, flocks of parrots burst upward from the dark teeming mass like an explosion of rockets. The monkey village yawns, fornicates, pinches, scratches, chatters itself awake. In honeycombed caves the glow-worms conglomerate starrily. In linked caves, between clotted stalactites, the bats hang themselves up together. The gentle pandas in their dainty dress indulge in party frolics among the rocks.

At sea it's the same thing: whales, porpoises, dolphins, flying fish, mackerel, sprats, all travelling in schools and shoals; oyster-beds packed to capacity;

animalcula and foraminifera swarming in astronomical multitudes.

Higher up the scale there's no difference either. The tribal community rouses itself *en masse*. Everyone begins laughing and talking and praying and crying and cooking and washing and working on top of everyone else. The baskets of the fighting-cocks are placed close together for company's sake. Paying the civilized penalty, Mr. Whosit awakens flimsily divided from the tens or hundreds of rabbits inhabiting his particular warren. Quick the switch and the dial, then, to bring loud the voices of nations; quick the collar and tie, quick the pants of respectability, the shined shoes to run to the crowded eating-places, the streets, the buses, the trains, cars, planes, offices, parks, night-clubs, theatres, hospitals, churches, graveyards, tombs.

Heaven. The populous scene partly suggests a fairy-tale illustration, partly a picture from an old-fashioned Bible, partly the enchanted cave in a pantomime. Broad brilliant azure sky with cloud cushions on which parties of angels recline. To the left, a landscape of flowery fields where numerous saints and seraphs are strolling about or sitting on the seats placed as if in a park. Fountains playing, birds singing, rivulets rippling. The grass is brilliantly green, the flowers sparkle like jewels, instead of bridges rainbows span the streams, the benches are made out of solid gold.

At the center, in tiered majestic gradations, there soar, enormously, steps of intense and dazzling white alabaster. Endless streams of angelic figures move in stately procession up and down this colossal stairway which presumably leads to the Throne.

On the right, seen panoramically at a lower level, a sort of huge skating-rink, blastingly bright and surrounded by dense gold-crowned, white-robed crowds. From here rises, very remote, very impressive, words indistinguishable, a vast volume of community hymn-singing with *vox humana* and massed bands accompaniment. When the communal howl dies away there is a sharp prolonged staccato rattle, something like a burst of machine-gun fire, as the saints pitch their crowns on to the glittering surface in front of them.

Now, at the extremities of the stair, appear seraphim whose lifted trumpets discharge notes in crisp upward cadence. The crowds on the right relax after their vocalism, break into groups, laughing and talking, and slowly begin to disperse. They give the impression of lighting up cigarettes, pushing their haloes on to the backs of their heads and then putting their hands in their pockets, although of course they don't do these things. While they are strolling away a band of children romp gaily at the foot of the stairs, playing touch-last with the cherubs, whose muslin wings are attached to their shoulders by braces of tinsel braid. The children are all about the same age, twelve to fourteen years old, sexually indeterminate, very china-dollishly pretty, with rosebud mouths and beautiful curly hair.

The little girl B (she is an unobtrusive spectator in the foreground) watches the children admiringly as they dance into the fields and begin making the flowers into chains and posies. (As each flower is picked another immediately springs up in its place.)

B is obviously very much charmed by all that she sees, although slightly overawed. She stands first on one foot and then on the other, looking all round, anxious not to miss anything, but not liking to move away from a bush which partly conceals her and is somewhat ostentatiously decorated with large silver twinkling stars.

The whole scene is humming with holy business, cheerful and social and sanctified at the same time; there is an audible hum too, the articulation of eternal, collectivized, innocent pleasure, a confused burble of music and distant singing; laughter, water, harps, birds, bells. Suddenly all this is stilled. Silence. A single bell chimes solemnly and with resonance far away.

The smiles fade from the lips of the angels, the saints break off what they are saying and look grave, the children stand quietly with serious faces, the flowers hanging down in their hands. Every head turns in the same direction.

B looks to see what it is they are all looking at. While she has been facing the other way, A has appeared from some unnoted point, and now crosses the foreground, dressed all in black. She walks not slowly and not quickly, but in immense isolation, utterly separate from the shining crowds, at whom, in passing, she glances without envy or interest.

Timidly forsaking the bush which shelters her, B steps forward, starts after her mother.

At the same moment, two executives of the angelic

order, severe in their robes, their faces shadowed by long pointed wings, advance, linked by a property arch which they carry between them. The arch, made out of gun-metal-colored paper (the sort in which silver is sometimes wrapped to keep it from tarnishing), simulates a subway approach and bears a small neon sign in red letters EXIT TO HELL.

Supported by an angel on each side, the arch is set on the ground. The audience looks uneasily from side to side, whispers flying about. A walks under the arch with a strictly impassive face: she seems not to notice where she is going. The seraphim at the foot of the stairs raise their trumpets. The saintly crowds shift, shuffle, whisper, stare, lean forward, expressions of deploring pietude glazing avid curiosity; stare, seasoning sempiternal brightness with the zest of distant but contemporaneous shade.

The first notes of the trumpets are blown.

Just as the angels are preparing to carry the arch away B makes a desperate dash at it and dives through.

Everything blacks out—as if in an abrupt dense smoke-screen—as successive curtains of darkness are drawn. The faces of the child-angels last longest, porcelain painted with Os of insipid disparagement. On the obliteration of the last doll face, the hymn singing, very distantly, starts up again and continues, diminishing into final inaudibility, for a few seconds more.

What happens when you start on the downward trip? The elevator doors clang shut, a suffocating infernal wind roars up the shaft, it seems as though you'll never get to the bottom; there's plenty of time to wonder what's coming and to wish yourself somewhere else. Of course there isn't a hope of ever getting out again into the light. Once you're on your way down the machinery takes charge of you, you're caught, trapped, finished for good and all. Certainly there are legends about individuals who have escaped, even after reaching the final platforms. But these are heroes, fabulous figures who perhaps never really existed except as projections of wishful thinking in the minds of ordinary people. At any rate, they are far too dubious and remote to be of any real moral support or to provide any justifiable basis for optimism. You might just as well give in and pluck the cruel thorn of hope out of your heart. It's always less painful to surrender to the stream of events than to turn yourself into a dam to be battered and pounded. It's true that if the worst comes to the worst you'll be drowned: but that's better than being beaten to a jelly; and there's always a slight chance that you may get washed ashore somewhere before the end.

And now, with regard to this drop into the lower regions, things really might be much worse. It's no good pretending that you get the gaiety down here. You don't get the variety or the excitement or the social or cultural life. If those were the things you were after you should have been much more prudent, you should have hung on to your original identity disk, number billion-billion-billion-whatever of the collectivists, instead of losing it somewhere or throwing it away in a fit of bravado. Then you could have trooped along to paradise with the rest and been one of the crowd for-ever-and-a-day. But since it's happened like this, since you've been thrown out on your ear by the celestial party, or thrown yourself out, it makes no difference which way you put it, the only thing left is to adapt yourself as well as you can.

It's lonely? Sure, it's lonely. That's what you asked for, didn't you? After all, if you hadn't been too superior for the gang, you wouldn't be here. And think how much more distinguished it is to be on your own, or with one or two individualists like yourself, than to be an ordinary gregarious animal going about with the herd.

You miss the sun and air? Sure, you do. There are some million miles of solid obstruction between you and the free place where the wind blows and the birds sing in the sunshine. You'll never feel the sun warming you any more. You'll never hear the birds. No bird could live in this atmosphere, this *ersatz* air that eddies here in stale and fetid artificial gusts. But you can breathe in it and like it too. And in the end it will smell sweeter to you than a sea-breeze, just as this dim, unvaried and unfresh light will suit your eyes better than the vulgar sun.

You don't like it here? Why didn't you keep out, then, for God's sake, while you had the chance? Anyhow, it's no good moaning and snivelling now. Put a good face on it. Be tough. Show the crowd you can take it. You're an individualist, aren't you? To hell with the crowd. What do you care about them? You're here because you've got no time for the crowd. What do you care about them and their damnfool heaven? To hell with heaven, anyway.

MY father thought I ought to be amongst other children, he sent me to a day school not far away. It was autumn. On windy days when I was walking to school each tree at the roadside stood in its own gold shower. I played a game catching the leaves as they fell. Whenever I caught a specially fine one I put it into my pocket. But next time I looked at it the colors had always faded and I was left with only a crumpled dead thing to throw away.

To begin with, I was quite glad to be going to school. I thought it might be something new and exciting. But it was not exciting, and soon it stopped being even new, and became disappointing and dull. There was a play at the end of term and I had a good part in it. I thought it would be a real excitement to act in a play. But when the day came that was somehow disappointing as well.

After that everything that happened at school seemed unreal and a waste of time, a part of the dull day world which was unimportant. Without understanding the reason, I knew that I had to keep the day unimportant. I had to prevent the day world from becoming real. I waited all through the day for the moment of going home to my night world, the reality which I lived in the secret life of the house.

IT'S A BEAUTIFUL spring morning somewhere in the South. This is a country which later in the year will be burnt brown and harsh, but now its first ardent response to the sun has flushed it with tender radiance. Soft sienna villages crown the hills, and in every village the church bells are ringing. The notes of the different bells drift and flutter and mingle as if flocks of pigeons with singing reeds in their wings were wheeling between the hills. From all the villages streams of gaily dressed peasants are setting out for the town. Some ride, some travel in carts pulled by lumbering flower-decked oxen, most of all are on foot. They pass through olive groves where the scarlet tulips wave wild silken flags in the thin grass. Like *vivas* the vines brandish new fistfuls of vivid green. The whole landscape rejoices, the carnival notes of the bells swoop festively through the brilliant air. The peasants are full of holiday gaiety; it is a celebration for them, a great day. They go along laughing and calling to one another and singing to the music of their simple flutes and guitars

towards the town where the great day has also dawned. By contrast with the traditional idyllic country scene everything here has a somewhat ominous look. Views, sliding into each other, of the streets and squares of this town; a medium-sized southern town. Sunshine illuminates it hard as flood-lighting. The streets, hung with garlands and bunting and unintelligibly sloganed banners, are all deserted. The main street slopes from a large public building with marble steps and balustrade down to a frontage on a glass lake. The lake frontage is planted with flowering magnolias. The boughs of the trees are black, stiff and shiny as if cut in patent leather, the flowers dangerously white and upspringing. (Do they recall to the dreamer another dream?)

From every doorway people can now be seen pouring into the streets: they come in a steadily advancing spate, filling all available space and still pouring on. There is a confused throbbing, trampling noise while they are on the move which, as the leading ranks consolidate into a dense crowd in front of the public building, becomes shot through with conflicting march tunes, bursts of clapping, singing, cheers; also with boos and shouts; with sharp distant stabs of shots, breaking glass, screams. The latter sounds are barely audible in the center of the crowd where enthusiasm is solid.

Certainly the princess doesn't hear them, she hears nothing but cheering voices, as she appears in her crown and state robes at the top of the steps. While she is standing there bowing, a glimpse through a broken window of soldiers entering a room where a man sits reading, paying no attention to what's happening outside. Brief fragmentary flashes of smashed spectacles falling; arm-banded arms wrenching and grinding together thin shirt-sleeved arms;

raised rifle-butt; open book on the floor, pages torn and defaced by huge muddy heel-mark. Then the man hanging slack between arm-grips, heaved through a door, slung into the crowd; shirt torn, tie twisted off, blood pouring down his face under limp lock of hair. The people against whom he falls pay no attention, their faces are not seen, they are just trousered or skirted bodies, some with worker's hobnailed boots, some with two-toned suède shoes or natty brogues or patents, some with tennis shoes, pumps, sandals or high-heeled slippers, which automatically trample him as he folds up between them.

The princess does not see this episode (indeed, it hardly lasts as long as a flash of lightning), she is looking in another direction. She is watching a group of villagers, late arrivals from the country, who are hurrying along the now empty waterfront towards the streets lined with soldiers where the crowds are collected. In their eagerness not to miss anything the peasants are almost running: yet they can't help stopping occasionally to admire the wonders of the town with faces of childish and delighted amazement.

Now that the child idea has been introduced it suddenly becomes apparent that they are children, the soldiers are children, the crowds are composed of children, the princess is a schoolgirl in a cardboard crown covered with gold paper.

She stands on the steps, smiling, enjoying to the utmost the acclamation of shrill childish cheers. But only for a moment. Her triumphantly straying eyes are quickly caught by an isolated moving shape, invisible to those facing her, the back view of a familiar dark-wrapped figure walking across the now vacant waterfront and rapidly passing out of sight between the magnolias. Deep in the girl's brain the conflict at once beginning shows in the swift movements of her eyes, back and forth, from the black-branched distant trees to the close shouting faces.

Almost simultaneously with the start of the struggle it's over, her crown tumbles off as she runs down the steps, sheers through the crowd of children, some of whom immediately start scuffling over the crown, which is soon torn and trodden to pieces between them.

AT the boarding-school I went to when I was older I felt unhappy, although to begin with I didn't know this. The place was ugly outside and inside. The rooms were noisy and cold and crowded and I was alone in them. Of course, I always had been alone, but this was different. I was alone now in a bad way, alone in a crowded ugliness without respite. There was always winter framed in the frozen windows. The winter light marched along barren hilltops. The metal trees could never have sprouted leaves.

I began remembering things that were far away and forgotten; the way the sun shone in another country. One day when I combed my hair in front of a mirror, my mother looked out at me with her face of an exiled princess. That was the day I knew I was unhappy.

ON A LARGE bare round table in vacuum a double-page photographic montage is outspread: the same sort of layout as in an illustrated weekly but scaled up to three or four times the size. Detail of plain white clock-face marking seven-thirty. Jigsaw of school buildings angled in light and shade to sharp abstract design. Very chaotic detail of cloakroom with hockey boots scattered in pure disorder: rows of basins patterned with dirty hand marks, odd ends of grimy soap-cakes; a tap left running, forcing a costive passage through half-choked plug-hole; sodden stained towel twisted and pulled to the extreme end of its roller.

Views of classrooms, high-windowed, impersonal: straight plain functional furniture; everything unnecessarily bleak, comfortless, un-aesthetic: battered textbooks, atlases, volumes of standard works—some upside down—overflowing from shelves, upon which such things as broken chalks, paint-boxes, indian clubs, dumb-bells, skipping ropes, are stacked too in hopelessly overcrowded confusion. Very close detail of grey mottled inkwell with viscous slime of congealed ink dregs coating the bottom. Beside it, on a shallowly grooved wooden desktop, two pens, one with glossy new relief nib and tapered blue holder which terminates in a small heart made of lapis lazuli; the other with wooden holder, splintered and much chewed, nib crossed and encrusted with dried ink.

A funereal black overmantel supporting two bronze rearing horses stiffly tugged at by muscular half-nudes.

Long dining-tables, spotted white cloths; bone, plated, wooden rings clenching unfresh table napkins; huge hacked joint of mutton with gravy congealing; dish of stone-white potatoes; round glass dish cross-glittered with highlights showing glazed fruit-halves like visceral segments.

Detail of a tall highly polished silver cup on its black stand, and of other shapes and sizes of trophies in various positions. Crossed and tangled in a spillikin pile, skates, hockey sticks, tennis rackets (with and without presses), cricket bats. A football-sized ball is shown just about to drop through a circular piece of netting projecting from a goal-post against a sky across which birds are flying. An expanse of grass, very short, flat and arid, girls in tunics and white blouses caught by their shadows in arrested momentum. Girls' arms, legs, torsos, in gymnastic poses with ropes, rings, clubs, parallel bars. Girls grouped formally on a stage. Girls' hands warming on the coils of radiators.

An isolated radiator, too narrow for its height and by suggestion inadequate, under a curtained window at night; the parsimonious curtains leave a four-inch gap through which a small moon quizzes coldly. Other curtains in dormitories hanging like corrugated fences white in strong moonlight or clumsily bunched behind iron bedrails. Cupboards crowded with identical garments, in drawers, on shelves, on hooks and hangers. Repetitive framed photos of parents on shared dressing-tables. Close-ups of some of these. They are all photographs of the same two people taken in different poses; a stereotyped rather sweet insipid woman's face, slightly faded, with much fluffy hair; a typical pukka could-be-military Britisher vacuously and complacently staring. Beds, or maybe it's one single bed with white honeycomb spread, reflected in mirrors *ad infinitum*.

A rough-grained worker's hand with black broken thumbnail grasping a rope; complementing it, under a glum sky, a bell swung at a steep angle, clapper outlined on sky. A small brass handbell on top of a pile of books, horn-rimmed spectacles and a fountain-pen alongside. The clock-face again. The hands are now rigidly rectangled at nine o'clock. A solitary electric bulb, very isolated and frangible, dangling from white ceiling under a cheap white saucer shade at the end of a dark cord on which two flies have settled.

B looks carefully and seriously at these pictures for quite a long time, leaning her elbows on the round table. She seems to be trying to make up her mind whether she likes what she sees. In the end she apparently makes a negative decision because she turns away from the pages and her eyes slowly defocus.

The uncompromising black-and-white of the dream reproduction now blurs and comes to a minimal pictorial distinctness. The whole quality of apperception is emotional rather than visual from now on. Everything appears slightly out of focus, as if seen through half-closed eyes: not exactly distorted, but sufficiently out of focus to produce a feeling of great remoteness and unreality.

First a series of calm sensuous impressions; all of a sort to link up with the ideas of warmth, sunshine, security, love; in the background a tranquil rocking, a lullaby, without any threat of discontinuance. The right feeling could be represented here by a deep-South crooning of the "Do you want the moon to play with and the stars to run away with" variety, provided that the actual black mammy association could be kept out of it.

Gradually materializing pointillist stipple of sunlight sifted through green leaves. Transparencies of huge criss-crossed emerald-green leaves of the sort used by natives as wrappings: frayed fringes of such leaves. Very idealized mild round male oriental face smiling its benign smile; his arms, hands, yellow fingers; his clever fingers drawing birds, flowers, fishes, leaves, on thin rice paper under moving shadows of leaves. Smiling, he lets the pictures drift away on the breeze; one by one they drift off and become real; the birds open their red beaks to chirp as they flutter away; the leaves attach themselves to a bush, the flowers distribute among them their purple and orange wings; the fish float for a moment on the stream's surface before they swerve into the water and disappear. The sun, the sure fountain of warmth and comfort, the man. The smiling yellow face of the sun-man, yellow fingers benevolently juggling the world.

Again the generalized sense-impression of friendly security with its background of peaceful rocking, wordless crooning, augmented this time by the reinforcement of some exclusive and unique support.

A woman with chrysanthemum-curly hair—it is A, of course—approaches from a distance and comes nearer and nearer; slowly and steadily approaches until she stands so close that everything else is shut out. Quietly bending her face neither mournful nor gay, she takes B's hand and walks away with her down a narrow path; receding with her along the private, blind, quiet, inviolate path, the backward-reaching, down-reaching tunnel, as if into the crater of an extinct volcano.

AT school the spell I had learnt in my parents' house was no longer sufficient: I had to discover another and stronger magic. At school there was only the day world which I refused to accept and which would not accept me either. I had to find some private place where I could be at home.

A BIG COUNTRY estate in the finest old-world tradition. Undulating parkland with plantations of great trees here and there. The trees are all perfect specimens, scientifically nourished and trimmed, there isn't a dead twig or a superfluous branch to be seen. It's the same wherever you look. Everything has been planned, protected and cared for down to the last detail. And you can see at a glance that this has been so for hundreds of years. The lawns which surround the mansion on the hill have been shaved by skilful scythes to the smoothest velvety pile. Huge clusters of grapes hang in the vinery, peaches and nectarines ripen on sunny walls. The flower gardens are awash with color and scent. In the walled kitchen garden the fat earth overflows like a vegetable cornucopia. Strutting pigeons display their fans on the roofs of stables where splendid blood horses are housed. Sleek hounds drowse at their kennel doors. In sun-speckled shady groves deer daintily roam the preserves they share with the handsome gamebirds. As if suspended in amber, fish hang in the clear streams. Swans steer their stately and immaculate courses upon a lake that with no less exactitude mirrors the passing clouds. Here are no savage rocks, no jungles, no glaciers, no treacherous tropical lagoons, no fantastics of the animal, vegetable or mineral world to startle or cause amazement

Here all is temperate and harmonious; enclosed, perfect, prearranged, controlled and known.

A man wearing the uniform of major in one of the better-dressed modern armies steps briskly into the dream foreground, accompanied by an orderly. He has a small dark pointed beard and carries the words Liaison Officer in gold on each shoulder. With stiff one-two military precision the following motions are carried out:

Major removes cap, holds it at rigid arm's length. Orderly takes cap with his left hand: with right hand places halo attached to long trailing flex on major's head: plugs in to point on floor. Halo lights up. Orderly hands dark leather-bound book to major; salutes; marches off. Major opens book (the word *Parables* momentarily legible on the spine); in crisp uninflected voice, as if reading orders for the day, reads:

Of course the first essential for a domain of this sort is privacy. It would lose its charm straight away if every Tom, Dick and Harry were allowed to come in and carve his initials on the tree-trunks and litter the grass with cigarette packets and paper bags and all sorts of refuse. There's no getting away from the fact that the general public must be excluded if things are to be kept as they should be.

Certainly it's disappointing from the angle of sightseers who may have come from the city in some hot dusty overcrowded motor-coach, to find such an inviting spot hedged round with NO TRESPASSING notices. One can see the point of view of such people and sympathize with their feelings as they peer through the fence at the cool tempting glades and flowery dells on the other side. What a perfect place for our picnic, they are doubtless saying to one another. And doubtless they feel indignant at the idea of an individual landowner having the exclusive right to enjoy this delightful spot.

But one must look at the other side of the picture as well. Isn't there something to be said for the owner whose whole life is bound up with the property and devoted to maintaining it? Surely he earns the right to his privacy. Especially as he is almost certain to be one of those extremely sensitive people, of an entirely different order from the ordinary run of humans, and totally unfitted to live at close quarters with them. Deprive him of his seclusion and you deprive him of everything: perhaps even of life itself; for it's more than doubtful whether his delicate organism would survive such a shock. I don't mean to imply by this that our landowners as a class are particularly asthenic or that their hold on life is specially weak. On the contrary, we have all heard instances of these gentry displaying astonishing fortitude in defence of the things which they consider valuable. They will go to the most extravagant lengths in such circumstances; whether it's on behalf of an ideal or something concrete. But without these value objects—and being private is certainly one of the most important of them—they seem to lose interest in the world and to retreat from it accordingly. It's as if they presented their terms to life, and, the terms being rejected, quietly and proudly withdrew from the scene, preferring non-participation to compromise. Not good enough for me, you can imagine some old squire saying with a half-humorous, half-sardonic inflexion, in face of an ultimatum. And then he will take his departure without any fuss at all, unobtrusively abandoning the stage. For how can he, for so long the sole proprietor of a vast demesne, lower himself to associate with the public in an existence of base competition? No, you can't expect the descendant of a proud race, with centuries of tradition behind him, to tolerate the desecration of vulgarians; and you can't blame him either if, before making his exit, he secretly destroys his dearest possessions rather than have them fall into the hands of the mob.

The trend nowadays is towards more and more collectivism. Of course nobody denies that the good things of the world should be equally accessible to all, and that the owning of property by individuals is in theory deplorable. But it seems to me that careful consideration should be given to the case of the landowners who, far more often than not, are hard-working, abstemious men of high moral principles. Taking a broad view, is it really the best policy to eject them summarily from the positions which they alone are qualified to fill? Qualified, what's more, not only by personal training but by all sorts of hereditary influences, the value and power of which are not yet fully understood. Admittedly, from the collective standpoint, an estate, no matter how perfectly run, is ideologically valueless unless it is accessible to the community. On the other hand, if such an estate is delivered over lock-stock-and-barrel to incompetent and inexperienced managers, it will soon become factually valueless too. Would it not be possible to evolve some system under which the *status quo* could be maintained—perhaps until the death of the present proprietors—meanwhile raising the educational standard so that the general public will be fitted both to administer the estates efficiently and to appreciate them to the greatest advantage?

The problem, at any rate, seems worthy of study. To my mind, a very real danger exists of irreplaceable treasures being lost to the community through the thoughtless vandalism of uninstructed persons, if all these great places are suddenly thrown open indiscriminately.

What happens when a crowd of holiday makers bursts into such a property? They will uproot plants and damage trees which have taken many decades to reach maturity; they will leave gates open, allowing valuable animals to stray and to ruin the gardens; inside the house no object will be secure. In an hour or so the work of generations of skilled craftsmen will be destroyed.

Don't think that I'm attacking the common people or condemning their high spirits. All I want is to make sure that they don't lose sources of future pleasure through receiving them prematurely before they have had opportunities of learning to appreciate their true worth. That's why I'm entering this plea on behalf of the old landowners.

There has been a tendency lately to speak of these men as dissolute degenerates, given to all sorts of perversions. Let me assure you that in my experience this is by no means the case. In the course of events I have come in contact with a number of them, and they have all been individuals of integrity and moderation, one or two even fanatically ascetic in their personal lives, although naturally their outlook is entirely different from ours. I don't want to appear as a partisan of the landowning class. Indeed, I am aware that I have already pressed their claims beyond the limits of personal prudence. But I would be dishonest to myself if I were to refrain from making a final appeal for serious consideration of the whole difficult problem.

While the Liaison Officer is reading the last few sentences a bell starts to ring, at first distantly, becoming louder and more insistent as the dream grows correspondingly more transparent. Finally he is seen closing his book, preparing to remove his halo, laughing spectrally for an instant, before he dissolves altogether with the disrupted dream.

NOW I understood why I had to prevent the day world from getting real. I saw that my instinct about this was a true one. As my eyes grew more discerning, I recognized my enemy's face and I was afraid, seeing there a danger that one day might destroy me.

Because of my fear that the daytime world would become real, I had to establish reality in another place.

TRUTH, it's everything. The man who said, What is truth? certainly touched on a big subject. The truth of the matter is that there's far too much truth in the world. The world, from whichever point you observe it, is altogether too full of truth. It isn't easy to recognize this truth in the first place, but it's impossible ever to ignore it once it's been grasped.

Every single possibility or impossibility is true somewhere to someone at some time. It's true that the earth is as round as an orange and as flat as a pancake. It's true that the wicked island goddess Rangda is a good goddess when she takes off her mask. Black magic on top, white magic underneath. That proves that black's white, doesn't it?

It's true that the idea of America is a bright and shining thing in the mind. It's true that the idea of America is a crude and brutal land inhabited by adolescents and gangsters.

Defeatism's true; war's true. So's idealism and the hope of a better society. You pay your money and you take your choice. Civilization's gone down the drain. Utopia's just round the corner.

It's true that civilization marches on: atomic energy plus universal war. The Hallelujah Chorus from Handel's *Messiah*; H.M.V. recording. That's a truth, although universal war. There's the truth that you go to bed with and the truth that wakes you up at three o'clock in the morning when the tigers are jumping up and down on the roof and eternity is flapping at the earth like somebody shaking a rug. There's the truth of loving and hating, being an extrovert and an introvert, a success and a failure, travelling all over the world, living your whole life in one place, having security, accepting all risks. Then there's the truth that you find with the dirty glasses stacked in the sink. That's a different sort of truth.

Books continue to be written in one truth and read in another. The radio announces various kinds of truth to suit every listener. Atomic warfare is true and so is the Sermon on the Mount. Truth is everywhere, in everything, all the time. That's why it's true. It's true that all this is obvious and has been said often before. That truth's as true as any other truth too.

The artist paints his picture to suit himself or his client. The artist. Yes, well, let's have a look at him now.

The artist. Traditional with beard, corduroys, big black hat, bohemian scarf. Or, if you prefer it that way, elegantly turned out in a thirty-guinea suit tailored by Simpson, Simpson, Simpson & Simpson of Savile Row. Anyhow, the artist. As a young man. Full of enthusiasm and theories and alcohol and amours. As an old man. Successful, and respectfully badgered by publishers for autobiography: or nondescript and obscure. Or forty and frustrated and amused-not-so-amused-by-it-all. The artist, anyway.

He turns his back upon Fitzroy Square and walks south down Charlotte Street with his slouching or affected, or jaunty or casual, or alert or pompous, or resigned or aggressive, or indifferent or weary step. Past the art dealers and the window full of rubber devices; past the delicatessen and the tobacconists and the sensational news placards (if not cricket results must be death and destruction tall on the placards); past the cheap restaurants, past the dirty curly-haired kids playing hopscotch. Past the dead tower (dead as all the dead days, Oxford or else Montmartre; dead ones, you who were with us in the ships at Mylæ, who had amaranth breath, who had death in the veins, dead living before the world died; dying now no longer); past the fabricators of steel candelabra.

Into Geo. Rowney & Co's. Or Winsor & Newton Ltd., Rathbone Place. It's really quite immaterial which because he can get any material that he wants in the way of material at either of them. Unless of course he prefers the products of M. Lefranc, in which case he may have to walk a little bit farther or maybe not if the truth were known.

As a matter of fact it isn't anything in the paint line that he's after just now. Not water color or oil, artist's or student's or decorator's, in any language whatever; so it's simply a waste of breath to offer him deep ultramarine, *outremer fonce*, *oltremare scuro*, *ultramar obscuro*, etc.

What interests him today is a good large sheet of Whatman paper with a fairly rough surface and not tinted any color at all: which he fastens upon the skyline with four drawing pins, *punaises* or thumb-tacks, according to the country he's in at the moment: and proceeds to apply a fast wash which runs down in a double-toothed dragon's back of black trees ridging steep foot-hills, iron-black mountains behind, down to the bottomless cañon of black-green water. A somber landscape eventuates, worked out in blacks and greys and the very gloomiest shades of viridian. A scowling sky, ominous mountains, water cold, still and solid-looking as ice, trackless fir forests, the fine spray from the gigantic waterfalls fuming slowly like ectoplasm. No sign of life, no living creature visible anywhere. Only the forbidding and desolate silence, deathliness, of this mountainous far-off region. Till suddenly bursting from the high crags, soaring and planing above the highest pinnacles, two great birds, eagles most probably, swoop together into an extraordinary and desperate aerial encounter; plunging down headlong together, and all the time reciprocally involved, diving through a thousand feet of pure frozen emptiness, righting themselves, it seems miraculously, at the very last moment before crashing into the water, to glide interlocked over the surface, without effort, without the faintest perceptible winging, at the culmination of their appalling love flight.

With a *dégagé* flip of the palette knife the paper's off and making way for a clean sheet. This time the artist has changed his style. No more romantic gloom, no more melodramatics. This time it's a street scene that's delineated; or rather, a part of a street scene, a shop window, a toy shop window to be precise, with a Noah's ark in the middle. Up the gangway the animals troop, there isn't an odd one among them, everything's in perfect order, not a single mistake, no two of the same sex, not even the earthworms, though heaven knows one might easily make a slip. Last of all Mr. and Mrs. Noah shoulder to shoulder and carrying between them a pair of huge indescent shells stuck together like jujubes. In they go, the doors slam, Gabriel sounds his horn, the lady evangelist with gold voice and armor-plated bosom breaks a bottle of champagne over the bows to complete the launching. Don't deplore the extravagance, friends. Replenishing the earth is no picnic, and it wasn't the best champagne anyway.

Not the incomparable Moet & Chandon Dom Perignon Cuvée of 1921; or the great Lanson of that same year; or the magnificent Moet & Chandon Imperial Crown English Market. Not even one of the 1928s; such as a Perrier Jouet, or a Pommery & Greno, or a Bollinger, or a Krug, or an Ernest Irroy, or a Pol Roger, or a Clicquot Dry England, or a Heidsieck Monopole.

Don't worry, folks, there's plenty more where that came from, could be magnums, could be jeroboams. The fashionable wedding breakfast's overflowing with gold-necked bottles in coolers, with orchids and caviar and diamonds and pearls and the creations of the most exclusive-expensive couturiers and the perfumes of a royal prince.

Don't ask awkward questions, comrades. Don't bring all that up again now. We've got to increase the population somehow, haven't we? Otherwise how are we going to keep on fighting everyone everywhere all the time?

Under striped awnings the wedding guests depart; in cars, in bars, they re-shuffle, re-sort themselves for the night. The old act is on: Boy meets Girl, at smoky parties, in public conveyances, in the best hotels, in the lowest boozers, in suburban parlors, on park benches, under viaducts. And steady trains of midgets march behind.

Off comes the paper again. And now the artist seems to be impatient. It isn't enough just to rip off the sheet and leave it wherever it happens to fall. This time he has to tear it into very small pieces, crumple the scraps in his hand, and throw them peevishly into the grate along with the cigarette ends and the empty cigarette packets, the spent matches, the paint rags, the flattened and finished tubes. Perhaps he's a trifle hung-over this morning. Perhaps the breakfast coffee wasn't strong enough; perhaps he really needed a couple of doubles to start the day with; perhaps there were too many bills in the morning mail; perhaps his wife walked out on him yesterday; perhaps he's just happened to catch the eternally calm clear eye of one of the Heaven-Born. Or perhaps it's one of a million other possible trials which accounts for the dissatisfaction he feels with his own efforts.

After all, they do these things much better on

the moving pictures. So let's turn to the dream screen, which displays simultaneously three superimposed themes.

The most remote of these presumably should be the one used as background, very frail, very underemphasized, ranks of uniformed figures marching on a diagonal slant from upper right to lower left. These figures are exactly similar, featureless, diminutive, uncolored, like the outline drawings used in demonstrating statistics. The ranks are evenly spaced, extending across the whole screen; they march throughout at a regular medium pace, raising their legs in a modified goose-step. The effect on the eye of this transient army is no more disturbing than a background of falling snow or continuous heavy rain. The background does not fade or solidify: it is not modified in any way by the development of the other two themes; nor is it ever extinguished by them.

Against the basic motif, moving roughly horizontally, but in a fluid, swerving, weaving band, a stream of dancers, men and women in couples, appearing small at left, gradually enlarging center (certain couples enormously), diminishing again as they move towards right. As the dancers individualize they are seen to be of all ages, classes and nationalities, stepping their various rhythms to a jumble of distant dance tunes further confused with intermittent far-off blaring of martial music. No face remains prominent long enough for complete apperception, but continually changing details emerge. A schoolboy in Eton jacket partnering a heavy fly-blown woman of fifty with bull-neck and sparse blue marcelled hair. A hard, judge-like man of about sixty-five, personifying the more hidebound and sadistic type of disciplinarian, woodenly placing his feet in bright patent leather shoes. Simpering over his stiffly encircling arm, a horribly travestied sweet young girl of sixteen in perfectly transparent white muslin; the rouged points of her breasts stand out through the white like the red spot on a tarantula. A poet-like, precious young intellectual, spectacled, wearing a silk shirt and otherwise a baby's napkin, is dancing with a big black negress whose far-too-tight satin dress is bursting at every seam. His twin brother, identical except that his face is redder and that he wears an eyeshade instead of glasses: in his case a striped and monogrammed blazer goes with the napkin. His partner a Peter Arno blonde with the usual trimmings. A dear old lady in white fichu and cap; her swollen ankles teeter dangerously over three-inch-pinpoint heels studded with brilliants. An overalled surgeon, sinisterly grotesque with his gauze mask and rubber gloves. A yellow gentleman flashing yellow diamonds. A bus-driver in uniform. A very dignified, polished, bearded member of the Académie Française attired in full *tenue de soir* with the Legion of Honor in his buttonhole. Fliers, bell-boys, witch-doctors, scientists, typists, waiters, beauty queens, parsons, racing cyclists, whores, sandwichmen, cooks, schoolmasters, prize-fighters, Chinamen, kings. These people can be rearranged indefinitely to include any combination, as they waltz or shuffle or glide or rumba or tango or walk or whirl or whatever across the screen.

The third theme has as its accompaniment sentimental song-hits of the most saccharine variety, which fragmentarily make themselves heard cross-jangling the other tunes. Equating pictorially, numerous quick flashes flicking about the screen with glimpses of conventional love scenes in gardens, conservatories; a girl and boy on a staircase embracing; an enlaced couple leaning over a steamer rail and watching the moon rise (moon is searchlight); mouths searching, clinging; hands (male and female) fumbling, stroking, clutching, questing, trembling, gripping other hands, bodies, slipping straps from shoulders, unfastening buttons; shot, from above, of a man and girl in bathing-suits pressed together in a tight clinch on a beach; close-up of the girl's upturned, imbecilic, nympholeptic face. Various erotic flashes, in boats, cars, bedrooms, parks, dance-halls, etc. None of the shots, which break out at random all over the screen, lasts for more than a second. The effect is rather that of looking at a high building in various parts of which windows are lit up one after another as lights are switched on and off in the different rooms.

Music increases to utmost confusion of dance bands, military bands, crooners, as something whitish, roundish, rises from center base and slowly travels straight up like a balloon, like a bubble, traversing the whole height of the screen. Maybe it's an igloo; maybe it's an egg. Up it goes, steady and sedate, and inside it B is sitting cross-legged, reading a book. Just as the bubble, the balloon, the igloo, the egg, or whatever it may be, reaches the top of the screen it explodes quietly with a smothered genteel belch.

The bubble-plop signals disruption of the combined themes. The dancers and lovers blow madly in all directions; fly apart; disintegrate: they and the music vanish together.

The ranked figures continue their unassertive march for a few seconds, until it becomes clear that they are quite young boys in some sort of uniform, Boy Scouts perhaps, or members of some other youth organization.

The troop of about twenty boys marches along a dusty road in full summer sun. The marching is not at all smart, several boys are out of step and others have broken rank and are lagging behind. They are all hot and tired and quite considerably bored. One who has a blistered heel scuffs along barefoot with his shoes in his hand.

At right, parallel to the road, from which it is separated by a wire fence bearing No Trespassing notices, a cool, shimmering lake with flowering flags growing to the edge of the water. A freshly painted row-boat is moored to a miniature jetty. Opposite this the march falters, breaks down completely, the boys straggle up to the fence, bunch together there like young cattle, eyes focused enviously on the boat and the water. Simultaneously with the break up of the march, from behind some willows on the other side of the fence, two smiling girls (one is unmistakably B—could the other be A in her younger days? It's impossible to tell really, they're so much alike) appear on the sunlit slope. Smiling into one another's faces, oblivious, self-contained, they walk hand-in-hand to the jetty, unfasten the boat, get in and row out and away, towards the center of the lake.

From the level of the boys' eyes, through the thick wire mesh, as if looking into a cage, the boat shown withdrawing swiftly, with extreme effect of solitariness, inaccessibility; diminishing into a toy, a waterbird, a floating leaf in the distance; vanishing.

OUT of my urgent need I found the way of working a new night magic. Out of the night-time magic I built in my head a small room as a sanctuary from the day. Phantoms might be my guests there, but no human could enter. Human beings were dangerous to me, like tigers prowling at large in the daytime world. Inside my secluded room I felt safe from the tigers I sometimes envied. Sometimes a savage beauty lured me into the sun and I would start to love the danger a little. On these occasions I felt the reluctant love drained painfully from me as blood drains from a deep wound. The tigers lapped my love's blood and remained enemies. The inhabitants of the day laughed at the gift I wanted to bring them, and I shut myself in my inner room to escape the betrayal of their arrogant mouths.

SOMEONE IS running madly up and down stairs. What devilish torment can hunt the poor fellow like this? No sooner does he reach the foot of the staircase (it's short, mercifully, but quite steep), than he turns and is off to the top as fast as he can go. Then down he rushes at once, almost tripping over his own feet in his crazy haste to get to the bottom and start climbing again.

So he keeps on, up and down, up and down, up and down, like a caged squirrel or a mouse caught in a treadmill. Such agitation is horribly painful to watch. One holds one's breath in suspense, waiting for him to fall badly and break an arm or a leg: or else his heart must surely give out and he will have a collapse of that kind. Already he's worn to a shadow, a wraith, whose features are too ghostly to be recognizable.

Each moment he grows more shadowy, more transparent. He's getting smaller and smaller too, as the altering dream perspective banishes him to the distance where, finally, his frantic restlessness is no more disturbing than the activity of a spider within its web.

Are these clouds or mountains which now blossom like huge flowers in the glowing light of the sky? They might even be figures, solemn supernatural beings, archangels or gods, with faces masked in their own radiance. Light steadily fills the whole dream until there's no room for anything else. Even the disembodied voice of the Liaison Officer can barely squeeze itself in, so that only fragments are heard of the lines he is reading about

the Blessed Genii who walk above in the light, gazing with blissful eyes of still, eternal clearness

The perennially clear eye of the Heaven-Born opens to a stare of shockingly bright moonlight. The eye is located at presumptive God height so that the terrestrial globe is seen as if from an airplane cruising over it at about three thousand feet.

A cold, steady review of night, moonlight, vastness, emptiness, loneliness, desolation, by the celestial eye. The bleak and enormous reaches of its vision swoop occasionally to focus detail at close range but never linger on anything. The eye is checking a record of silence, space; a nightmare, every horror of this world in its frigid and blank neutrality. The actual scope of its orbit depends on the individual concept of desolation, but approximate symbols are suggested in long roving perspectives of ocean, black swelled, in slow undulation, each whaleback swell plated in armor-hard brilliance with the moonlight clanking along it; the endless, aimless, nameless shoreline, flat, bald-white sand, unbroken black-tree palisade; the heavy and horrid eternal onrush of breakers sullenly exploding their madness of futile power, millions of mad tons piling, booming, collapsing, swirling in chain-mail mosaic of mad moon splinters; blanched mountain range a ridge of clenched knucklebones.

The eye sinks slowly to travel at tree height past clattering black slats of palm leaves knife-edged on steel;

and looks at a hideous fanged stone idol in front of which lies a hyena, gnawing away at a lump of half-rotted flesh; dips lower to inspect three strung human skulls dully ululating in wind; rises again to medium altitude and directs its impassive scrutiny towards death-white ice-caps; towards hopeless vastness of dreary continents crawling with pestilential rivers, scabbed with plains in the corners of which perpetual dust-storms are festering; towards blasted battlefields and ruined cities running with seared putrescence; over dead village roofs and poisoned gardens, broken walls bitter in snow or moon, blank windows black with nothing.

And so on, in regular and perfectly unflinching survey

which non-dimensional B from deep within its pupil coincidently shares

until a fresh manifestation gathers itself together, and focuses interest on:

the castle the sun

The sun is, in fact, just on the point of rising over the town. This is the precise moment when Day and Night are balanced before exchanging their spheres of influence. Low in the left segment of sky the full moon still shines white on steep gables and eaves, and glazes window panes behind which people are still fast asleep in their beds.

People are in bed too in the houses at the opposite

end of the town where a faint preliminary pink is spreading fanwise out of the east. But it's noticeable that the sleepers here are restlessly stirring, already beginning to break away from their dreams. The moon retires with graceful prudence, her blue train trailing behind, switching slickly over the horizon before the roguish rosy-fingered retinue has time to twitch at it. Up swaggers his majesty in the spotlight, adjusting the gilded curls of his peruke, tossing his daily largesse with elegant gestures of careless munificence, flicking the golden flakes from his laces like snuff.

As the first gold strikes the weathercock on the castle tower the sleepers waken, throw off the bedcovers, jump into their clothes. All in an instant the life of the morning's begun: white smoke puffs briskly out of the chimneys beside which storks are tidying up their nests; eggs and bacon sizzle in frying pans; steaming coffee pours into over-sized flower-patterned cups; the cheerful clatter of breakfast things all over the town is punctuated by the double knocks of postmen going their rounds. In next to no time all these things happen: and then the school bells start ringing, children with satchels and apples come tumbling and chattering out of the many doors, crowding the narrow streets which are crowded already with people going to work, with market carts, with street-sellers putting up stalls, washerwomen carrying bundles of linen, dogs pulling handcarts, priests hurrying along with rosaries or small black books in their hands. The day's well established before you can turn round. And now all the workers are busily employed: a drone of voices comes from the schoolhouse windows; housewives are knowingly prodding the provisions set out in the market or haggling with stallholders; in steamy washhouses, women up to their elbows in suds shout jokingly or crossly to one another; the dogs are panting in the shade of their little carts at the end of their task; the priests are closeted and anonymous in solemn confessionals.

From high up in the castle dominating the town B watches these activities somewhat dubiously. There's a section of flat roof which forms a sort of terrace between two turrets, and it's here that she's standing looking over the parapet beside a clawed gargoyle which has melancholy human eyes in its pig's face. It seems to be a whimsical, jolly, busy, toyshop scene that she's looking at: except that, like all horror-dream backgrounds, it's a bit too harmless to be truly disarming. It's very innocence gives it away. Such emphatic innocuousness is bound to contain a submerged threat. The threat never comes completely into the open, but is concealed in isolated glimpses and incidents, trivial in themselves, yet generating a growing sense of tension, anxiety, apprehension.

For instance:

An open window behind which, in the shadowed room, indeterminate worrying movements are faintly discernible; a hand suddenly comes out, grabs the window shut and snaps down the blind.

In a small public garden, watched by a few idlers, men with besoms and long-handled rakes are making a bonfire of leaves; and this is only remarkable because it's summertime and the leaves haven't started to fall yet.

A neatly dressed man with a bag in his hand is hurrying along the street to the station. His arrival is timed very well as the smoke of the train can be seen in the distance just as he gets to the booking office. But then, instead of buying a ticket, he suddenly walks out of the station again, takes a piece of chalk out of his pocket, marks something on the door of one of the neighboring houses, and hurries off in quite another direction.

B isn't looking out for incidents of this sort: in fact, she's hardly aware of having observed them at all, being consciously preoccupied with the general pattern of which they are only insignificant details. Nevertheless, she is influenced by them without knowing it, they are responsible for the vaguely disturbing background of uncertainty in her mind.

Presently there's a new sound, a noise of cheers and clapping, approaching the castle. A famous ballerina is driving through the town in her open carriage, the people in the streets recognize her and acclaim her as she goes by. B leans over the parapet to look. She has an excellent view, the carriage is driving right up to the castle entrance. It's a fine carriage, polished like jet. The horses are beautiful, glossy, spirited creatures. They slow down as the coachman tightens the reins. Yes, they are actually stopping just below the place where B stands. A flock of pigeons which has been circling around the turret simultaneously alights in the street. As if for some prearranged purpose, the birds assemble all round the carriage and the prancing horses.

The fair-haired ballerina looks up and waves her hand. Come down here, she is calling to B. Come for a drive in my carriage and I'll show you the town. Her voice carries like the sound of a bell.

B does not move. There's a violent conflict inside her. She longs to go down to the famous dancer, she's longing to see the sights of the town at close quarters instead of looking on distantly from her tower. And yet something is holding her back, warning her not to venture out of the castle.

Come down, come down, the ballerina calls again and again.

All right, I'll come, B answers finally, overcoming her hesitation. Wait for me. I'm coming immediately. Please don't go on without me. I'll be down in a moment.

The pigeons fly up to her as she hurries away, they flutter about her, filling the air with their wings so that she can hardly see where she is going. A sound something like a groan comes from the gargoyle, which laboriously raises its claw in a gesture of restraint or appeal. B is far out of reach already: she does not see the movement or the stone tear which slowly and painfully extrudes from the gargoyle's eye and rolls down the length of its pig's snout.

Soon she's climbing into the carriage. And how glorious it is to be careering along behind those spirited horses at the side of the ballerina. It's all wonderful, like a new world; the speed, the excitement, the applause, the hat-raising, the salutes of the passers-by, the privilege of being the envied companion of the subject of such universal admiration. The town, too, takes on a new aspect from this angle. The streets, which B is accustomed to viewing in foreshortened perspective, seem much finer than she had supposed them to be. Even the crooked lanes leading to the poorer quarters promise adventure and mysterious revelations.

The ballerina points out new wonders at every corner. Look, look, she cries, and when she raises her arm the sleeve falls back like a calyx and new marvels reveal themselves. A girl has come to the fountain to fill her bucket with water; but as the carriage rolls by diamonds, emeralds, sapphires spout from the dolphin's mouth, in a second her pail is full up with precious gems, a whole fortune flashes into the bucket in one beam of light. The ballerina laughs. The sound of her laughter is like bells ringing out from the hilltop. B seems to have heard that sound of bells in another place.

Look, look, says the dancer again. In every window-box of the house they are passing the flowers come out with a rush and fling their bright petals down, showering the carriage and its occupants with scented confetti.

Things like that keep happening continually. But now the horses are racing so fast that B doesn't have time to catch more than confused glimpses of what's going on. The speed at which the carriage is travelling makes her quite giddy and she has to cling to the edge of the seat to keep from overbalancing as they swing round the corners. Far, far overhead in the burning blue sky the pigeons are flying, keeping pace with the horses whose wild hooves clatter frantically on the paved street.

Too fast, B calls out, I'm missing everything. Can't we go a bit slower?

She's really a little nervous. Supposing one of the horses should slip and fall, or the carriage upset or run over somebody? It seems only too likely to happen.

The dancer just laughs. Probably she didn't hear what B said in the rush and noise of their progress. She at any rate doesn't seem in the least anxious. Her yellow hair blows out in the wind as if a fire lighted her laughing face brilliant with power and joy.

Suddenly the astonishing drive is over. Rearing and slithering, the horses are pulled to a standstill. The carriage rocks dangerously; and before it has become steady, the ballerina darts out like a bird, her feet in their green slippers fly up the steps of a magnificent building outside which an equestrian statue threateningly brandishes his great sword.

Where are you going? Wait for me, B shouts, getting out of the carriage as fast as she can. The dancer doesn't answer or look round. Perhaps she doesn't realize that B has been left behind. Perhaps she has suddenly forgotten about her.

In desperate haste B starts climbing the steps in pursuit. It's no good, though. These steps up which the green shoes flew like birds B's feet can only scale slowly and with infinite labor and pain. Each single step towers in front of her like a wall and she can only drag herself to the top of it by putting out all her strength. Her feet too feel hopelessly heavy and out of control, seeming, as they do sometimes in fevers, to belong to somebody else or to be weighted with heavy stones. Once or twice more she calls out to the ballerina. But already she's lost hope, she knows there won't be any response; the dancer has vanished behind the huge mounted knight who looms in between them.

Besides, B is really too exhausted for shouting. It's as much as she can do to draw breath at all. She stands quite alone now among the hostile faces that have collected around her. The crowd which previously waved and cheered with such enthusiasm has all at once become angry, threatening, morose. These people in their dark clothes watch her silently, like a herd of dangerous beasts, occasionally shifting their positions, or muttering, or exchanging ugly glances between themselves. They do not make any overt accusation, but B understands they resent her presence in that place, she has no business to be there and will be made to pay severely for her trespassing. What the penalty will be she hasn't the faintest idea. But it's only necessary to look at those heavy, lowering faces, at the same time stupid and vicious, like the heads of treacherous animals, to know that no brutality is out of the question.

Very slowly the crowd is closing in on her, edging forward almost imperceptibly, but always decreasing the space which is her precarious safeguard. Panic-stricken, B's eyes search wildly in every direction, without discovering a solitary sign of hope. Above her, sheer as a cliff, the blank façade blots out the sky. Like an implacable and denunciatory finger the long black shadow of the knight's sword points to her over the heads of the crowd. The carriage has silently disappeared from the street below.

A rumble such as might herald a natural catastrophe, a tidal-wave or an earthquake, comes from the onlookers who are all together murmuring the same fatal indictment, as, with obvious intent now, they draw in their constricting circle. B is like a mouse in a trap. She spins round, first one way and then the other, hardly knowing what she is doing. In one place the ranks of bodies seem less compact, she imagines that it might be possible to force a way through at this point, and dashes towards it. At the same moment she feels herself falling, the whole vast stairway collapses disastrously beneath her. With a great rush of wind the pigeons whirl down and beat all about her with their strong wings, bearing her along between them

into a small room with no windows or doors visible. The walls are scrawled over with dimly seen occult symbols, pentacles, wands, swords, etc. There are shelves of books; and a few phantom-glimmering shapes of vases, or urns. B sits on what might or might not be a narrow bed, reading by the light of four candles in a cross-shaped holder. It's very dark. The candles shed a flickering, limited ring of light over B and the open book and a part of the dusty stone floor, leaving everything else in shadow deepening to blackness in the corners. Here and there round the walls faint traceries of signs or letters come and go as the four flames waver. Absolute stillness. Hush. At approximately regular intervals B's hand moves to turn over a page.

After a time a vague stirring, thickening, in one of the dark corners: nothing so definite as movement at first: it's more a sort of concentration of tension in that corner. From which tenuous chrysalis presently emerges a second B, B's *doppelgänger*, materializing out of the shadows; coming nearer the light although very similar, with similar fair curled hair, discernibly older, wearier, more assured, more disillusioned; in fact, of course, A. Who, standing behind B, looking over her shoulder (B is unaware), remains for a while apparently reading what she is reading. Then, moving across the room, gradually departs from the scene in a reversal of the procedure by which she lately arrived.

Simultaneously with her dissolution, a faint sibilance starting, not from any special point, but emanating from all over the room, very subdued, seeming as if it might be voiced by the four walls or by the ceiling and floor. A rustling, a susurration, like blown leaves, in which now and then some reference to danger becomes incompletely distinguishable. This sound continues from now on, principally as an indeterminate rustle as of water, leaves, wind, occasionally clarifying itself into the actual word Danger or one of its synonyms. B, without actually hearing, is not oblivious, because whenever the word becomes recognizable, she looks up or makes an unquiet movement. Finally she jumps up, glancing nervously round the room, pushing her book away so that it strikes the candle-holder, rocking the candles and sending waves of light alternating with shadow in confusing sequence, like pages turned rapidly back and forth.

At the same time the whispering loudens to ordinary speaking pitch, to clamor, to shouting, to utmost volume, as near deafening as possible, of voices chaotically shrieking, together, separately, interrupting, competing, with increasing speed and intensity, such phrases as: Danger, Keep Out; It is Dangerous To Open The Window; Danger de Mort. And so on.

The earsplitting pandemonium is suddenly shattered; into long dry grumble and growl and intermittent snapping and cracking of bursting timbers, crumbling masonry, as the whole structure of the room collapses inwards, obliterating B in a heap of amorphous wreckage, rubble, from which thick clouds of dust are seen blowing upwards like spray. This, under blank moon as before, the celestial eye transiently takes stock of, passes on.

WAS my mother afraid of the tigers? Was that the theme of the music she danced to with death in our quiet house?

When I went home between the school terms I was still alone in those rooms where nothing had altered. It was the same then as if I'd never been away. My mother's sadness and boredom still lived in the house with the shadows and the grey rain on the windows. Their presence accompanied me as I took my unspoken questions from room to room.

Sometimes I had an impulse to ask my father about the things which perplexed me: I watched him and waited for the right time which never came. My father always seemed to be in a hurry. He was like an important stranger with no time to spare. He made decisions for me about practical things, he directed my life, and when he had done what was suitable he forgot me.

At school and at home it was the same; I was alone. This I accepted and knew it would always be so, wherever I went, and whatever happened to me. There was no place for me in the day world. My home was in darkness and my companions were shadows beckoning from a glass.

THIS-TIME it's not just the voice but the visible presence of the Liaison Officer which opens the dreaming eye. He's reading again from what looks like the same book (although one can't see the title), but the details of his appearance have altered, he is bareheaded and wears a white garment—a smock or an overall—on top of his uniform. The chief alteration is in his manner. He's no longer sure of himself, his voice sounds uneasy, his expression is puzzled, and he keeps glancing anxiously out of the window where there's a distant view of a castle floating mirage-like in the mists. Except for the window and the major himself, there's nothing much to be seen in this great gloomy old hall. Everything's ghostly and grim and dark, and though there are people present, they seem to be in another dimension. All that's perceptible is a continuous vague stir, as if a crowd of transparent onlookers were seated in thin air, fidgeting and whispering, rustling their spectral papers and shuffling their unseen feet.

It's enough to make anyone reading aloud feel nervous: especially as the atmosphere generated by these invisible spectators is far from friendly. There's a sort of malicious tittering in the background: a nightmare Alice-in-Wonderland inconsequence, which is most disturbing. The inconsequential element is manifest too in certain architectural caprices and light shifts, whereby the building is given a fluctuating resemblance to a church, a law court, a prison, an operating theatre, a torture chamber, a vault. That the major is more and more affected by these metaphysical stresses, is evident from the increasing tension of his manner and voice as he reads:

An instance of how misunderstandings and estrangements can occur between relatives:

B wants to talk over some obscure point with her father. She has probably made several efforts to approach him already, but without success. Her attempts have up to now been always inopportune; perhaps made at a time when he was on the point of leaving for his office and, already a few minutes late, could not possibly delay his departure any longer. Or perhaps she spoke to him when he had just come home after a hard day's work on some specially intricate and abstruse official problem and was too tired for talk. Or else, when other circumstances were propitious, an important message to which he was obliged to attend may have been telephoned through from the department by one of the under-secretaries.

Today she makes up her mind to ask him at breakfast to fix a time for the conversation. At the regular hour she goes into the dining-room only to be told that her father ordered his breakfast earlier than usual and has left the house.

B decides to follow him to his office, a journey which, travelling on the suburban train, normally takes about forty minutes. This morning, although no warning is given of any alteration in schedule, the train not only takes over two hours on the way, but finally deposits its passengers at a terminus in quite a different part of the city, from which she is obliged to make a complicated bus trip, involving several changes, to reach her destination.

When she gets there, in a state of nervous anxiety after all these delays, a secretary informs her that her father has gone to lunch at a certain restaurant which she knows quite well. The man is friendly and sympathetic, he is anxious to help her, he is certain that if she goes at once she will catch her father before he has finished his meal. B thanks him and hurries off as fast as she can. But in spite of the fact that she's perfectly familiar with this restaurant, has herself been taken there several times, she is unable to find it. Various passers-by of whom she inquires the way give her conflicting directions. In the end, a policeman tells her that demolition work was started some days ago on the building which had recently been classified as unsafe.

Rushing back to the office, B arrives there just in time to see her father getting out of a car in front of the entrance. He pauses to say something to the driver. B calls out and starts running towards him. Her voice is drowned by the noise of the traffic; and, at that instant, by the sheerest bad luck, a whole lot of people, jostling one another in their anxiety to board an approaching bus, come crowding along, getting between B and her father who crosses the pavement quickly in front of them. B has no time to catch him before he disappears through the door which a saluting porter swings open and through which she is never allowed to pass. She sees the car glide away. She sees the door close. The situation is hopeless. The only thing left for her to do is to go home again.

This time the journey takes no longer than usual. But at the house it transpires that her father has already been and gone; he must have driven home in his fast car immediately after she saw him, having found that he would be obliged to undertake a business trip to another city and wishing, since they had not had many opportunities lately of being together, to see B before he left. She hears that, having made the long drive, for which he could barely manage to find time, on purpose to say goodbye to her, he was naturally rather put out to find that she was not in the house and that his time had been wasted. He had actually waited half an hour, expecting her to return. At last, as there was no way of knowing how long it would be before she put in an appearance, and as his own business was urgent, he had gone off looking cross and aggrieved. In fact he had left a message to say that he was most disappointed and upset about the whole matter.

Very distressed at the way her good intentions have gone wrong, B consoles herself with the prospect of getting the entire complex straightened out as soon as he comes back. But then she remembers that he will not be returning until the following week, and that by that time she herself will probably be away from home.

Once more the suburban house THE ELMS, the

desirable residence. The trees have grown slightly taller. It's raining. Saturated soft lawn, like a green sponge; black tree-trunks glistening with rain. The wet brick walls of the house: the paint on the doors and window frames is less fresh than it used to be; but this would hardly be noticeable.

A general view of the house in its trees, roofs of adjacent houses appearing on all sides through the trees. Tree-tops are doleful in grey and cold douche and drench of rain; leaves are bent under weight of raindrops, tipped, freed and weighted again; the roof, the whole slant of tiles, swims under a thin film of water, rain slithers thinly to gutters, gurgles in pipes and gutters, trickles from vent-pipes, seeps into sodden earth. Raindrops spatter a puddle beside the porch. A blind taps on a half-open window its untranslatable message.

Now inside. It's no particular season or time of day. The rooms are chilly, somewhat dark because of the dark sky reflected in windows steadily blurring with rain. The recent thud of the front door perpetually hangs suspended in feeble blind-tapping, rain noise. Most of the rooms are unoccupied. Outmoded and unloved knick-knacks haunt the dusted drawing-room with desolate derelict neatness; the oriental boxes empty, the fretted sandalwood fan folded in exile. Encamped behind the closed kitchen doors two women servants, shut off with cups of tea, gossip and sip; they seem unconnected with the rest of the house; nor is the house affected by their presence there.

Solitary B wanders aimlessly from room to room.

She is making a tour of boredom, loneliness, monotony, dullness, although she's not conscious of it. In room after room the rain filming on all grey windows; gloss-hard or padded gentility of heavy furnishings; genteel formal masculine room, smell of telephone, leather, tobacco; aloof genteel dining-room glinting of silver.

B finally goes to her own room, stands for a minute fingers drumming the window-pane swimming in rain, then sits down on the bed, opens a book.

The book opens with a thud of the front door. Contemporaneous with this sound, the hurried suggestion of a man dressed in dark business suit and carrying a dispatch case, leaving the house, getting into his car, driving away. The empty rooms of the house filled with rain noises, dullness, nullity, the morse-tap of the blind; closed in the kitchen, the two prim-faced servants, apart in their closed world of picture papers and tea.

B turns the pages. Each one is exactly the same as the one before. She turns them faster and faster, running them over between her thumb and first finger, speeding them up into a bioscope blur, the door thuds spraying out quick like gunshot pellets. When she comes to the end she closes the book

and puts it down on the seat of the railway carriage. The train is just roaring into a tunnel. B looks back, through the transparent coaches and baggage car of the train. Far behind, very small, framed in black circular tunnel mouth, diminishing at great speed as the train rushes the opposite way, the suburban house wet in its trees, rain still greyly slanting.

At the terminus all is noise and confusion. It's a great cold dingy place full of bewildering hustle and shouting, escaping steam-hiss, whistles and clanging bells. Everyone is in a terrific hurry: gangs of people dash wildly in different directions, loaded with all sorts of impedimenta, piles of books, bags, overcoats, boots and shoes, food, mascots, pictures, pets, awkwardly shaped wooden objects, bats and rackets, boards and unwieldy globes, which they hurriedly deposit in various places. But no sooner does one of the groups succeed in getting all these things arranged in some semblance of order than, in obedience to whistles, bells, shouts, the whole collection of articles is snatched up again to be bundled off to some other position where the process has to be gone through afresh. To add to the general confusion, loudspeakers are continually bawling out orders or directions of some kind, while, only slightly less loud, other unamplified voices seem to be reciting or chanting, and still others are carrying on shouted conversations with friends. And as if the jumbled parties helter-skeltering this way and that didn't create sufficient disorder, isolated individuals keep scurrying among them, forcing their way in the opposite direction to their neighbors, leaping down from the tops of piles of boxes or scrambling to precarious perches on high window-ledges, perhaps in search of a missing companion or a piece of lost property, the subject of their incomprehensible shrill inquiries.

In the midst of all this turmoil B is quite at a loss. Someone who seems to be in authority has called out to her to join a certain group, which group she doesn't hear, and before she can ask for more information the person who gave the order has disappeared. B looks round hopelessly. How in the world is she ever going to find her right place in this bear-garden? Nobody seems in the least interested in her. Nobody seems to care what she does, where she goes, what becomes of her. It doesn't seem to matter to anyone whether she moves or stays where she is all day long. People are constantly bumping into her and pushing against her with their clumsy paraphernalia, but not one of them can spare a moment to stop and answer her questions. Occasionally an individual, better-natured than the rest, will call back before vanishing some muddled instructions, of which B cannot make head or tail—particularly since only a word or two is audible in the tumult.

She really begins to feel desperate. The people here are all so rowdy, so scatterbrained, so intent on their own higgledy-piggledy affairs, that it's useless to try to catch their attention. And then the place is so huge and dreary, and every part of it is so much like every other part, that to find one's way about in it seems an impossibility; to move in any direction is almost certainly to get lost among the hurrying crowds, the stacks of indiscriminate objects which are for ever collapsing as something is dragged out from the bottom, and then being chaotically heaped up anew.

Still, she can't stand in one place indefinitely, to

be jostled and pushed from one side to another. Without any aim in view, simply because there's less of an uproar this way, B moves in a certain direction. For some reason or other there are far fewer people here, the main throng suddenly seems to be concentrated elsewhere.

Soon she's in a quiet space, by herself, in front of a door which is evidently not meant to be opened, or even to be seen, because it is painted exactly as if it were part of the wall. However, it does open quite easily when B turns the handle, and she goes through it on to a narrow platform above a stage

where a ballet of the Graduation Ball type is in progress. The platform is flimsy and small, balanced on scaffolding up there in the wings as if perched on enormous stilts. B advances timidly to the edge of it and looks down.

Level brilliant light on the stage, warm colored; from the footlights and in a strong generalized flood (not spotlights) from high up above. The auditorium is merely suggested by a receding tide of shadow beyond the footlights. No orchestra visible. The ballet music is stimulating: it has much gaiety, freshness, without sugariness; it has "a curious perfume and a most melodious twang".

The dancing master in black satin knee-breeches and buckled shoes leads his class, which consists of about twenty boys and girls in equal numbers. The boys are dressed in fancified cadets' uniforms; strapped long white trousers, gloves, colored monkey jackets with silver or gold buttons and touches of lace. The girls' costumes are more varied. Some wear full muslins, just over knee-length, a cross between ballet skirts and the usual young girl's white party frock; these have wide sashes made of stiff silk with fringed ends in sharp naïve colors tied in large bows behind. One or two are in period dresses, bustles or crinolines with display of lace pantalettes. Others wear fantastic versions of conventional school clothes, lustrous velvet jibbahs, candy-striped guimpes. Accessories, such as gold corkscrew-curled wigs: ropy gretchen plaits held by flat ribbons; demure chenille snoods; fans; openwork elbow-length lace mittens, black, white or colored; bronze or black dancing sandals, crossed ankle elastics; block-toed ballet shoes in different satins.

Across the stage, to lively four- and eight-bar strains, the pupils dance in double line, girls ahead, following the master who is leading them with brisk yet dignified steps. Then pirouette and back with the boys leading and the master an agile black grasshopper in the rear. He waves his brittle arms like antennæ, tattoos his buckled shoes in dry rataplan on the boards.

Now to different rhythm, in spaced mock-formal advancements, uneven numbers, one, pause, two three, pause, and so on, the girls sedately skip into the center, take places on frail spindle-legged gilt chairs set by powdered and liveried menservants for each one as she approaches.

All sit, feet crossed, hands folded, in identical poses of mimed modesty.

Then the boys, all together in tin-soldier military

formation, march up, left right, crisp rap-tapping meter, halt, click heels, stiff toy-soldier salute, each in front of a chair.

Girls rise.

Footmen swiftly and silently remove all chairs except one, which is left standing in the exact middle of the stage.

After prim exchange of bows, curtsies, partners dance off together, steps and deportment very hypocritically *comme il faut,* under the stern supervision of the master who mounts the chair and from this eminence critically watches the class, scrutinizing each couple in turn, occasionally giving a defaulter's shoulder a smart rap with the baton which he uses to beat time to the music.

The dance, which starts off with so much decorum, gradually begins to lose its formality as the tempo quickens. Covert smiles and whispers, arch looks, spread from one pair to the next, relax into more and more open mischievousness, frivolousness, flirtatiousness. The dancing master scolds, reprimands, works himself into a frenzy, hitting out left and right with his baton, all to no purpose. He rapidly loses his dignity, loses control over the class which will not pay attention to him any longer. He becomes a figure of fun. The pupils, girls and boys, laugh and mimic him, dodging his baton as they pass by. Finally a boy snatches the baton away, dances off brandishing it mockingly. Another boy tilts the chair, tips the master on to the ground. Now more than ever like an irate grasshopper he hops among the revolving couples, chattering with rage, ineffectually trying to recover his precious baton, his symbol of authority, impotently striking promiscuous fist blows which are warded off with derision.

Feet fly faster and faster. Skirts spin faster and faster. The dance develops into a kind of age-of-innocence orgy in the midst of which dervishes the black insect-like maestro, frantically flinging in all directions his stick-dry limbs that appear to be on the point of snapping off from his body.

Down into the midst of this comes B, her green slippers seeking in time to the music the rungs of the ladder leading down to the stage. The music has gone to her head as well as her feet. Without any reserve she darts in among all those twirling dresses, those flying curls, those slapping braids, on eager toe-tips shuttling between them, soliciting every couple in turn. But no one surrenders a partner to her: and she is obliged to perform with the dancing master a feverish *pas de deux*, the pair of them oscillating vertiginously, caracoling, glissading: she in search of a partner, he pursuing his puissant baton which is passed by the dancers from hand to hand, tantalizingly flourished before his face, tauntingly tossed away.

At last, to crashing tumultuous chords, the fantasia terminates. But music immediately takes up again on a delicate dawn motif, very limpid, young, pure; an aubade.

With dainty tripping rustle of petticoats, brisk scissor-crisscrossing of white trouser legs, the dancers retire to the back of the stage where chairs are now arranged in a wide crescent; girls settling themselves with bird-like preening, flirt and flutter of hair, skirts, fans; boys sitting on the floor or leaning on the backs of the chairs.

Out in the center the master, B and one danseuse who did not withdraw with the rest of the class, are dancing the tentative opening phrase of a new movement which develops the rapprochement of the two girls under the maestro's ægis.

The dancing master has unobtrusively regained his baton and with it his dominance. Depended from his thin fingers, the baton swerves delicately in time to the music as he dances, inspiring the dance of the girls. Their four green shoes move complementarily about three feet apart. Up to now the quality of the music has been predominantly ethereal, and this feeling the dancing girls, in their spacing apart and traditional formalized posturing of head and body, also convey. It is still aloof and airy as possible, but now superimposed on the initial morning simplicity of the theme are certain elusive suggestions of provocativeness, ambiguity, as the girls approach one another more closely, touch hands, finally become linked together in their gossamer intrication.

They glide hand-in-hand in front of the master. While he grows steadily taller they both lift their identical pairs of eyes slowly and seriously towards his face, into which they look questioningly for a moment, heads tilting back to focus him as he towers upwards: then their eyes lower, sliding without dubiousness sidelong to meet each other; they look into each other's eyes for a moment; simultaneously and very slightly and briefly they smile, and circle dreamily in exact imponderous harmony, and, with a lacing of buoyant arms, embrace one another's waists.

The master's head has reached up to the roof. His hair is the roof, the illumination of the stage pours out of his eyes, his thighs are gigantic buttresses shoring the building. From his fingers dangle the puppet strings. For a few seconds longer he manipulates them, jerking the green feet back and forth, propelling and twitching the rigid arms. On gilt chairs the abandoned puppets (they are like bright scraps hoarded for a patchwork quilt that have been carelessly turned out of a workbag and left in disorder) have fallen this way and that; backwards with legs in air, sideways across one another, forward with heads on knees, heads on to floor. The puppet master drops the remaining strings; the last two dolls, collapsing, droop over each other's shoulders with stiff arms outstretched; a monstrous, dry, horny hand descends on them, pinches one negligently between thumb and first finger, lifts it up out of sight. The lights go out. And though "There's nothing more" remains unsaid, grey draughts of emptiness drift from the stage.

THINGS at school began going wrong. I broke rules and was often in the detention-room. People started saying how difficult I'd become. Generally they were angry with me, but occasionally one of them spoke kindly and asked questions which I wouldn't answer because I distrusted kindness. Once a doctor wanted me to tell him what went on inside my head, but I didn't trust him either. I wouldn't talk to him in case he was on the enemy side. How could I know that he wasn't one of the tigers?

How could I explain that school was a machine running by clockwork, and that it was because I didn't *fit* the machine that I was always in trouble? At the start I had tried to *fit* in. Now I'd stopped trying because I knew it was hopeless. I knew there was no place for me in the day unless I gave in altogether, and this I was determined I wouldn't do. The daylight world was my enemy, and to the authorities of that world who had rejected me I would not submit. They had insulted and damaged me and I would never surrender to them.

A MUCH enlarged presentation of a pile of forms on a flat surface under a window. The pile is seen from the side, very monumental in the strong light, as if made of stone. The effect is somewhat that of a model cenotaph squarely set on the dark featureless plane. The top of the pile is in full blank-white, flat-white daylight. Cold white light edges the edges of certain projecting forms, striating the black-shadowed perpendicularity in a way suggestive of steps or of sharply jutting relief.

A very clean large ringless hand approaches the pile. It could be either a male or a female hand. The practical fingers have squarish shortish neatly trimmed nails. The flesh of the hand shows tallow-white against ice-white paper.

The hand hovers momentarily; sinks; the thumb moving *glissando* along the edge of the topmost form, fingers curving above, till it reaches the corner; first finger smoothly descends and in co-operation with thumb raises the paper slowly upwards: holds it vertical for a moment (the words EXAMINATION RESULTS, and CASE NOTES, come alternatively and fugitively into focus heading the form): lowers it to horizontal position on smooth dark surface.

The paper now seen laid out flat on the surface, of which only a narrow border appears framing it, with the mass of piled forms rising steeply behind, top of the pile is out of sight. A huge highly polished black fountain-pen like a gun-barrel is trained on the paper; the glittering nib over the black ink-feed carries a dazzlingly brilliant bolus of light on its rounded tip.

Discharging brisk light-volleys, the nib travels judicially down the left side of the paper where a sequence of printed categories is set out with appropriate sections for comments: halts opposite CONDUCT near the top of the form; after hesitation proceeds at reduced pace downwards to SYMPTOMS; pauses again.

The fountain-pen poised like a gun taking aim. This position is held while, very distantly, a bell begins ringing. On the last stroke of the bell, nib, jabbing brilliance, is sharply directed to paper which it contacts with a short crackling explosion.

Immediately, light and sound condensing, concentrating into, respectively, the voice and nimbus of the Liaison Officer (restored now to his original smart dress and assurance), who reads from the original spine-titled black volume, in his original dry, precise, expressionless, military tone

The Terminus Clock

Choosing a clock for an important terminus is a serious matter. It's not a question that can be settled offhand, like buying an alarm-clock or a wrist-watch, in the course of a brief visit to the *horlogerie* round the corner. No indeed: this is a totally different affair, and one which may easily require years of research and consideration. Just glance for a moment at the various aspects of the problem. Let's start off by asking ourselves what are the essential qualities that such a clock must possess. First and foremost I imagine everyone will agree that it must be an accurate timekeeper. When it is remembered how many urgent matters—matters literally of life and death, to say nothing of vast business transactions and state operations—depend on it, there can be no doubt that everything else must be secondary. As long as there is any integrity left in the human race there will be also the desire for an impartial standard of accuracy. That being decided, however, we are only at the start of our difficulties. The concept of accuracy is not static; it is, on the contrary, constantly fluctuating; a clock which keeps perfectly good time for us may be quite unreliable for our neighbor, and indeed for us too on another occasion. So in whose hands are we to place the decision? It might be best (if we could establish a majority) to trust to a majority judgment. But that is not feasible. The probability is that the very people who are most unanimous today in their opinion will tomorrow be all at loggerheads, and each come hurrying with some new recommendation of his own to supersede the previous common agreement.

Such obstacles paralyze one from the beginning, and so it may be advisable to pass on and to think less about the mechanism of the clock than of its design. Here again every section of the community will want something different: practical people being most likely in favor of functional plainness, while the æsthetes will demand an artistic presentation. And these conflicts will be further subdivided among themselves into minor clashes; as, for instance, in the case of the artists, between the so-called moderns and the academicians, and then into still finer distinctions, impressionists versus pointillistes, symbolists versus surrealists, *etc. etc. ad infinitum.*

Even supposing that by some arbitrary move the clock has actually been installed in the terminus, this, unfortunately, will only lead to fresh strife and fresh complications. Factions are sure to complain that the wrong site has been chosen, the clock-face, besides being of an unsatisfactory shape and size, is either too high or too low, or else is improperly illuminated; that it can only be seen with difficulty from the waiting-room, and not at all from behind the bookstall, and so on. On top of this there comes the technical problem of servicing the clock and maintaining it in first-class running order without in any way interrupting or interfering with the general routine functioning of the terminus as a whole.

When all these things are added together one begins to recognize the probably insuperable difficulties of the undertaking, which all the same can't possibly be abandoned. The long patient hours of thought and study which serious-minded people have devoted to it all culminate in a longing for the time when the thankless task can be concluded and put away, like a difficult book the contents of which have been mastered. And for that reason the terminus clock is represented by students as being composed of sixty metal sheets, one for every minute of the hour, which fall and cover each other successively like turned book pages.

The Liaison Officer is seen for a second beneath a huge station time-indicator, closing his book, in the act of turning away, as the dream changes.

A harsh metronome clicking, getting gradually louder until it reaches the loudness of the snap of a medium-sized dry branch repeated at three-second intervals. Now with each crack a rectangular plane, describing an arc, rising, falling, horizontal, in the fashion of a series of loose leaves held together at their bases, or of the type of clock that marks each minute after the hour on changing indicators. All ephemerally exhibiting pictures of doctors, civil servants, professors, government officials; making reports bent over desks or tables. The high-heeled shoes of a typist and her rayon ankles twined round a chair leg; a group of white-coated workers comparing case notes.

With abrupt speed-up of clicks to one-second spacing the turning leaves distinguishable as college, hospital, government forms snowing into a pile. It is not possible to read what is on the forms (most of the printing is just a blur), but on one or two of them B's name is legible, on others single printed nouns appear as: AGE; QUALIFICATIONS; CLASS; DESTINATION; ATTITUDE TOWARDS; RESULT: with the beginning (indecipherable) of a written comment.

Suddenly a precise disembodied voice asking coldly: Have you any statement to make at this stage?

Followed, after slight hesitation, by the voice of invisible B; at first stammering, scarcely audible; gaining gradually force and tension until it breaks on an overtone of hysteria.

By what judgment am I judged? What is the accusation against me? Am I to be accused of my own betrayal?

Am I to blame because you are my enemies? Yours is the responsibility, the knowledge, the power. I trusted you, you played with me as a cat plays with a mouse, and now you accuse me. I had no weapon against you, not realizing that there was need for weapons until too late.

This is your place; you are at home here. I came as a stranger, alone, without a gun in my hand, bringing only a present that I wanted to give you. Am I to blame because the gift was unwelcome?

Am I accused of the untranslated indictment against myself? Is it my fault that a charge has been laid secretly against me in a different language?

Is my offence that I stood too long on your threshold, holding a present that was unsuitable? Am I accused because you, wanting a victim and not a friend, threw away the only thing which I had to give?

Immediately after B's voice fading, the metronome click speeding up to crazy haste, papers storming down in frantic acceleration; men's, women's voices (some with foreign accents), pedantic voices, affected, bourgeois, professional, authoritarian, etc., voices;

speaking all together, from all sides, in confused unrelated comment, all with somewhat derogatory tendency, from which only a few phrases emerge with any comprehensibility or consecutiveness. As

B does not concentrate. . . . Does not adapt. . . . Does not co-operate. . . . Does not compromise. . . . Not satisfactory . . . unsatisfactory. . . Does not. . . Un. . . Dis. . . Does not. . . Non. . . Un. . . . Not. . . Non. . . No. . .

BY the time I went to the university I had become more skilful in my dealings with day. The secret the rain had whispered to me years before, the secret of living apart from the daylight world, had now taught me to avoid conflicts without endangering my seclusion. Working from my hidden base in the dark, I warily reconnoitred the territory of the light, and described what I found there.

In all the chaotic violence under the sun, I saw only more cause for distrust and withdrawal. But now I was stimulated by danger, changing my anxiety into written words. I relied on what I wrote to build a bridge which could not be cut down. It was my own self in which I trusted, not seeing self as that last cell from which escape can only come too late.

HAS THE blissful eye lost its clearness for once? Can it be suffering from an attack of migraine, or what? The outer fields of its vision still remain fairly clear, but the center, where attention would normally tend to focus, is occupied by a dead spot, a blur of no special color or shape. Extending and underlying the pathological suggestion, the outlying images are all of a nature to accent the ideas of confusion, danger, violence, chaos, strife.

The extreme periphery concerned with colossal cosmic disturbances, fiery birth-throes of planets and the cataractic dissolution of globed systems on a scale too shattering to be more than hinted. An angry pulsating miasma of bloody red suffuses all this as though the capillaries of the eye were deeply inflamed.

Drawing in somewhat, the scenes moderating to terrestrial proportions, but still uniformly disastrous, world-wars, ruinous sieges, plagues, famines, appalling contests of atomic weapons, vaporized and dissolving cities, whole continents exploding in flame, universal torture, destruction, death.

Contracting again, approaching the fringe of the central blur, certain pictures emerging in much greater detail. First, details of cracking, toppling masonry and structural damage so close as to resemble earthquake fissures; leading with more distant and now unequivocal view to the disintegration of a city after atomic bomb hit and to the presentation of the ultimate vaporizing preceded by its upflinging a strange and fancy mushroom in the sky. Also establishing, beyond human destructiveness, the appalling blankness and the intense oppositional indifference of the cosmos.

Followed by glimpses of one and then of several abandoned cages of a travelling circus, and the stretched jaws and skeletal midriff of a starved tiger fighting the bars of the cage, the landscape behind rainswept, a road crammed with panic-stricken refugees, vehicles stogged in mud, overflowing the bounds of the road.

A sudden spuming oil-well, ignited, horrific flame fountain; another one blazes up; a mammoth warplane; a mischievous boy's face grinning as he releases death; the smashed city; the current familiar pathos (whatever its up-to-minute form happens to be); domestic ruin, broken-up homes, toys, etc. A beautifully delicate and pure fan of water from a burst main spraying a bloodied arm-stump among avalanched paving blocks.

A few more eye views: they are conceptual rather than actual, symbols of global violence in the opening mind.

A high wicked barbed-wire fence in hard sunlight, the small mad eyes of the barbs glinting with murderous brightness. Close behind the fence, an undersized, emaciated, intellectual type man, no special race or persuasion, peering through the powerful elaboration of wire in which he is caged. He wears a ragged, collarless shirt and torn trousers; stands with the somehow irritating pathos, the masochistic, slightly stupid, sadism-provoking nervous defiance of the predestined victim, myopically peering through the inevitable badly cracked, clumsily mended spectacles. There is the inevitable large bruise on his jaw. The inevitable shout cracks out and he jumps violently, drops his defiance as a handkerchief drops, spins round, and shambles off at an awkward trot.

From far away down the center of a dark street-crevice between huge skyscrapers, a small group of men and women appear unevenly, wearily marching: they are slight, poorly dressed, insignificant, utterly dwarfed by the monstrous size of the buildings. Rows of indignant, indifferent, glum or frightened faces watch them from the curb; but these hastily fade out before the arrival of a troop of giant policemen. A thin batlike whimper flitters between the enormous walls as the demonstrators are clubbed off the street.

Now an elderly middle-class couple pottering along the sidewalk arm-in-arm. Both are neat, frail, not well-to-do, intensely respectable. The old lady carries a shopping basket, the old man is using his umbrella as a cane in his free hand. They look like two old people up from the country as they advance, glancing timidly at the buildings and the crowds who hurry past without noticing them. Finally they come to a halt in front of tall ornate closed double doors where the word BANK is visible on the scrolled ironwork. The old man approaches and reads a small placard which hangs in the middle of the shut doors; his mouth slowly drops open; he stands staring at the notice for a minute, not believing, not taking it in;

then comes back bewildered with unsteady gait to confer with the old woman. The inevitable brutish-faced armed policeman beside the door watches them in scornful aloofness, swinging his truncheon. After a while the old man pulls himself together, steps up and says something to the policeman who, cynically narrowing his eyes, dribbles a few words out of the corner of his mouth almost without lip movement. The old fellow lingers in dazed appeal until the other's callous attitude dawns on him; drifts forlornly back to his companion. They stand side by side, dumb, as if lost or stunned, while rain starts to fall and the policeman looks on, leaning against the door-jamb. The old man becomes aware of the umbrella he is holding; then of its use; his hands twitch at it paralytically; he unfurls it at last and automatically raises it over the old lady's head; takes her arm again; vaguely leads her off through the rain. The policeman looks after them, swings his truncheon, moves farther back under shelter of the portico; yawns.

Immediately after the departure of the old people, a few yards up the street, a girl hurries out of a doorway. Turning to wave good-bye to someone behind her, she runs towards a bus which is approaching the stopping-place, slips, loses her balance, trips over the edge of the wet curb into the road. A cruising taxi squeals into a ghastly skid just as it is upon her, the driver pounding a frantic yowl out of his horn. A high shrilling momentarily punctures the traffic roar, cuts off sharply. One or two people start running; others shove and crane between the umbrellas to see what has happened. The policeman saunters up heavily, scattering everyone with the swing of his huge bruise-blue shoulders, swinging his truncheon.

The dream closes in to the central dead spot.

With delayed, lingering uncertainty this is disclosed as perhaps a web spun with grey mist-fibres of involution; perhaps a carcinoma; perhaps some sort of transparent maze. As uncertainty concentrates, involution honeycombs into greatest possible number of hexagonal cells on pyramidal base. As the honeycomb crystallizes, the cells quickly expand, differentiate; involution, now occupying the entire visual field, defines into . . . catacombs . . . ? hospital . . . ? prison . . . ? town with antique northern buildings.

Narrow streets, spires, quadrangles, stabilize cool in still grey light; so peaceful and so extremely quiet, remote, that they seem suspended in crystal. Calm in soft pigeon-colored stone, overlooking a lawn formal with spaced mulberry trees, a gothic façade pierced by slender windows, old, secure, rigorously remote. Figures stroll in and out of doorways, cloisters, with very faint droning accompaniment of academic discourse, distant sporadic chimings of clocks and bells. The speakers' voices are subdued, their tones unhurried, unheated, their cadences falling. Brief snatches of talk; such topics as the abstract entities, Wren's interiors, the migration of wild geese to Spitsbergen. Presently a more sustained ringing, bell-sounding from the high towers, reverberates with gentleness and solemnity. The figures continue to move up and down for perhaps half a minute longer: then quietly drift away.

The secluded scene is disintegrating, is blurred out, it reverts to the dead spot: the town is dissolving, it amalgamates with the dead spot (so that there is here, suddenly, the blank central eye-blur again): only the perimetral area is pulsing now at ominous speed and with the ominous growing tension of tom-tom beats steadily increasing in tempo though not in loudness.

This the dream college points with the man behind the barbed-wire hunted by more and more panic, running more and more awkwardly, undirectedly, his glasses falling, his eyes screaming out of the horror of his foredoomed and sweating face.

Glued to his face, biting it to bloody bits, now presses the turgid mouth of a great thick black salivary-shiny gun: the megrimed retina pulps and gushes into the dead spot spattered with brains and buttons and the grey blur still pumping.

Clear but very dimunitive vision across the convulsing of this man-spattered supcropticity, a quadrangle, empty, under watery cool clean evening sky. Lighted windows appear one after the other.

Which is being stored up? Which is being selected? Is it a quiet précis of monastic routine unwinding its neutral and satin-smooth spool of days snarled by nothing more serious than the easily unravelled knot of an examination?

Perhaps one could find out in some textbook ?
perhaps the Herr Professor would be able to tell us ?
Does the brain choose the images to be retained ?

Or does the memory rest on a psychological trestle that can be pushed in any direction ?

At the instant of balance, when the scale trembles between the polarities of night and day; what is it that returns ?

The light rain showering in sunlight while we sheltered under the archway; and went on over green velvet grass, between mulberry trees: and strapped books on the carriers of bicycles or piled them in baskets fixed to the handlebars, on our way to the evening, to drink coffee, and to talk for hours.

And when we were sentimental, standing in front of the house where he used to live, the poet, the tears came in our eyes, and we were uplifted. We said to one another, We too will write beautiful words, we will be remembered. And we felt uplifted. While you are young you have splendid pure feelings. Afterwards it's different, there are various euphonic substitutes.

Which are the prints to be pasted into the album out of the jumbled snapshots ?

Traveller on the world's oceans, in waking do you know the sea which rocks your temporary bed, or whether the shadow of the tropic bird or of the stormy petrel sidles across the deck ? There are certain pictures which did not fade or get thrown away Look at the pictures quickly
And you will catch your morning bird soaring above the towers, you will see your shadow fly over choristers and midsummer morning bells from the tower at the bridgehead.

There was a poem written for me on my comb;

written very small with the nib of a pen used for mapping. And when we drifted in the punt, late, in the backwater, I combed my hair, and I was Orlando, I was not man nor girl, and I was Ariel, drifting between the worlds, and a poem in my hair.

I do not know why I must keep these pictures small eyes, mad eyes that should have been starry the lovely danger waiting beneath the lime tree or faces cheating as they pass by, frozen for ever in their fraudulent smiles with the clocks striking an uncounted hour masks

Why this one ? Or that ? How chosen ?

Inexorable self, carried like the superfluous and tiresome piece of luggage which it is impossible to lose; franked with the customs' stamp of every frontier, retrieved exasperatingly from the disaster where everything else is lost, companion of the dislocation of cancelled sailings and missed connections, witness of every catastrophe, survivor of all voyages and situations. . . . I

FEELING more confidence in myself I was able to feel almost at home. At the university I met for the first time people who seemed to be of my own sort because their interests were like mine. These people could not be tigers, surely? They smiled at me, they wanted me for a friend; how could they be on the enemy side? I almost trusted them. But a barrier always stood between us, preventing friendship. I didn't know what this barrier was. Sometimes I thought my mother's shadow divided me from everything that went on in sunshine. I had only learnt how to be friends with shadows; it might be too late to learn the way of friendship in the sun.

Later I was thankful the barrier had not fallen. I found out that these people were not what they appeared; they were different from myself although they spoke a similar language. They were traitors who had betrayed their dark and magical origin for a cheap citizenship of the day. When I discovered this my confidence vanished, I felt afraid and ashamed. It was a terrible disappointment, a dreadful humiliation. When I saw how nearly I had been tricked into an alliance with traitors, I hid myself away in my secret room where no treacherous sight or sound could deceive me again.

HOW LOVELY the summer country is with flowers. The simple country flowers, pure colored and innocent, fill the air with their sweet freshness that is like a message telling everybody to be happy and good. Whether you go up on to the hills or down to the plain the fragrant message breathes all around you. Between the thymy aromatic cushions on the hillside, peals of harebells are soundlessly chiming. Under the burning green of the young beeches, bluebells spread a coolly translucent tide, and the wood anemones hold up their airy cups on stems as frail as the antennæ of moths. In the disused chalkpit at the foot of the hill the last primroses are lost in the long grass, together with wild white violets, themselves the color of chalk. A small confetti of many-colored stars trims the deserted track leading to the marshy fields where the plovers nest and fritillaries and king-cups stand up among the reeds. Milkmaids and cowslips share the meadows with daisies and buttercups; in the lanes, the hedges are spangled with dog-roses slowly turning pale in the sun.

As if to make sure that no one misses the goodwill that the flowers are everywhere distilling into the air, the birds have taken over responsibility for making their message vocal. Surely nobody could be impervious to the gay fountains of song that hundreds of invisible larks are spraying towards the sky? To say nothing about the music which comes from the thrush ambushed in lilacs, or the unearthly treble thread of the willow-wren.

The flowers and the birds between them, helped by the sun and the pleasant light breeze, have made a natural paradise which it is impossible to imagine as being invaded by anything evil or cruel or frightening or even sad. And to crown all this it must be a fête day as well. The low grey tower of the church, so old that it seems to have sunk into itself under the weight of the centuries, is now enlivened by the gaudy brightness of flags. Flags are fluttering over the vicarage and the manor and the school and the post office and out of the cottage windows.

The inn at the foot of the hill has other decorations besides the large flag the shadow of which dances over the grass outside. Wreaths and garlands of flowers, as well as fresh branches and colored streamers, are fastened above and around the two open doors and the porch and the squat bow windows. Some agile person has even climbed up the pole of the inn sign and fastened a great loose bundle of honeysuckle to the iron scrolls supporting the board upon which a nameless rural artist has painted the likeness of some heraldic beast. The inn itself is a long low mellow building that seems to smile. And it's quite right that it should have this smiling look because it's the center of all the gaiety, the headquarters, so to speak, of the message which the flowers and the birds have been spreading so diligently ever since the sun rose on this happy morning. Inside, a lively bustle of preparation is going on. Just now the doors set invitingly open don't reveal much except high-backed settles and white sanded floors: but from time to time one catches a glimpse in the background of a figure hurrying past with a tray of good things, hams, cheeses, fruit, or a basket of crusty loaves hot from the oven, indications of the feast to be served later in the day.

At present all the activity centers out of doors, where a sort of impromptu pageant seems to be going on. Under the chestnut tree on the green a number of benches and tables have been set out, and here people are sitting with tankards of cider and ale, an audience for the panting, beaming maypole dancers with their whirling smocks and ribbons, and for the group of children who are singing a folksong in reedily cheerful disunison.

The black-coated clergyman, like an approving sheepdog, smiles at the innocent antics. And a party of local gentry also looks on from the platform festooned with meadowsweet and with white, pink and scarlet may.

To the left of the platform, among other young people, a girl in green shoes is holding a great dog on a leash plaited with vivid cords. It looks as if she and her companions, with whom she is laughing and talking, will have some part to play later on. They stand there together with faces of excited expectancy; and the dog seems to share their pleasure, as he flourishes his whiplike tail and prances in anticipation.

The children's chorus falters unevenly to a close. Flushed and gasping, with a jingling of little bells at their ankles and wrists, the dancers laughingly troop away from the pole around which their variegated ribbons are left tightly twined. The audience claps, mugs are banged on the tables, a waitress in a check apron comes out carrying in both hands a huge foaming jug, the clergyman hurries here and there with directions and praise. For a minute or two the green is in confusion, before what must surely be the turn of the girl with the dog and her friends.

But she, all at once, at this critical moment becomes *distrait*. Her eyes wander. She is not looking any more at what's taking place, but at something everyone else is too preoccupied to observe, a woman in black who is slowly coming towards the inn from the direction of the churchyard. Slowly but steadily the stranger comes on, unnoticed, and taking no notice of anything. She does not look right or left and her face is not seen. She walks as if meditating, with bowed head, and with hands loosely linked at the ends of her long black sleeves. In the sun a sapphire flashes blue on her finger: it is the only color she wears anywhere about her. She slowly passes the green, making for the road that leads upwards into the hills

followed at a little distance by B, who lets the dog's lead fall and, unobserved by her companions, slips away through the crowd, in the wake of that dark and impassive form.

Come, they said, the co-operators, the false ones. Come and sit with us tonight, we are having a friendly discussion (to fit the universe into pigeon-holes), quite informal of course, and a nice warm kiss, at sunrise, to finish the party. There will be a place waiting for you. And this sweet brew which contains soothing syrup is something to warm the cockles and to make you cosy. Let's be cosy together. Draw the curtains. Make up the fire. Don't look out of the window. Why do you want to look out? It's dark and cold out there, so let's settle down to be comfy and to discuss the shadow of Emerson's Man.

Night time: a spirit of festivity is again in the air. And though it is not the idyllic Arcadian gaiety of the pastorale but something more sophisticated, more artificial, still there's an atmosphere of expectancy and joyous excitement gleaming from the eyes of street lamps and lighted windows. In fact it is a city of lights, the whole dream is ablaze with light, the whole sky is one vast shimmering aurora borealis of reflected brilliance. It's impossible to tell whether the stars are out or whether the moon is shining. All one sees in looking over the housetops is a diaphanous aerial curtain of wonderfully blended hues, red, orange, yellow, green, blue, indigo, violet, the whole spectrum extended and repeated from horizon to horizon like an endless series of rainbows in tremendous array. And on top of this, as if such a display wasn't dazzling enough, over the glimmering folds of the resplendent light-curtain, strange wavering bands of pure white luminosity flicker and weave strands so incandescent that they appear to be glowing with limpid fire.

It's really too much of a strain on the eyes, one can't look upwards for long. Not that there is any contrasting dimness below. The streets are as bright as day, for the numerous street lights on normal duty are for this special night reinforced by countless additional flares, torches, links, blazing braziers, relics of ancient times which have perhaps been preserved and stored for the purpose of being resurrected on occasions of this sort. Nearly every window, too, seems to be pointing its burning finger into the night; for few people have thought of drawing the curtains.

At the palace a state ball is in full swing. The great building, with every window aflame, rides the night like an enormous ship, isolated as it is from the glaring streets in a dim sea of encircling gardens where only the fairy-lights show a pale luminous phosphorescence among the trees and the sleeping roses. It is tempting to linger in these cool shadowed walks drowsy with the heavy scent of night-stocks and tobacco flowers. Hidden away at the edge of a lily pool is an arbor where the glow-worm globe silvers the cheek of a gardenia and the folds of a lady's gown. Accompanied by the faintest rustle of silk, a pair of lovers drifts past the little statue who holds up his cornucopia full of a pretty paleness of flowers or snow.

But here is the wide sweep, deserted now, where recently arriving guests thronged beneath tasselled awnings; where still the guards stand frozen in their grand uniforms, the powdered lackeys no less immobilized beyond.

There's no need to describe the splendors of the palace; the statues, the winging staircases, the columns, the balustrades of marble and onyx and agate and porphyry. What's the use of talking about the grandeur of the ballroom, the elegance of the dancers, the skill of the orchestra? Such things are better left to the imagination so that everyone can fill in for himself such details as he finds most satisfactory. Just as we can all picture the magnificent banquet overflowing with choicest wines, fruits, rare dishes of all descriptions, *sanglier*, sturgeon's roe, peacocks stuffed with peaches, or whatever seems most delectable and exotic.

Only as regards the ballroom it is necessary to mention the elaborate chandeliers (if that is the right term with which to describe these sparkling crystal confections of ice-bright lights, fantastically crown-shaped, and pouring an absolute flood of brilliance upon the scene). It is these amazing illuminations which give the ballroom such a unique distinction; for they are quite unforgettable; and a person who has once seen them is not likely to be much impressed by any other wonder encountered in his travels about the world

which makes all the more surprising the potency of the attraction   that draws the girl with the glistening green glass slippers to leave her partner standing thunderstruck immmediately under one of the radiant crowns   in order to follow a silhouette darkly beckoning and window-framed in the sapphire recessive night.

And so on: in considerable repetition, with varying detail, of the basic situation; the central theme itself being subject to variation in so far as the attraction is not inevitably to darkness from light.

For instance; the dream travels, quite briefly, through a picture sequence in which each view lasts only just long enough for apperception before it is superseded.

At first there is seen, from some distance away, a small one-storey house near the edge of a forty-foot cliff, at night; it is not very dark. The shut box of the house, with snaky convolutions of surrounding tree-trunks, is at the top of this picture: the rocky cliff face (below it the tarry water) is the crucial center. Next a glimpse of the interior in which (in bedroom with drawn blinds) an indication is made of someone asleep in bed: the indication further extended to suggest B. Quick shift outside again to the night sky pricked with a few stars. Huge storm-clouds gathering, expanding, immediately eat up the sky and its stars. The sea rising: the heaving sea-mass bursts into white horses; the wind lets fly; the wind pitched so that its noise is too the hissing spray blown from the breakers which now are filling the dream picture. The cliff is black shadow. A wave crashes; against the rocks the waves hurling a deadwhale-deadweight of water; the spray unfurls its enormous fan; the rocks quake amongst rush and lather and foam of retreating water; their stubborn, drowned, again battered, not yet quite smothered heads (did they really tremble?); upthrusting spray jets higher and higher from the successive breakers. Terrific waves swelling; huger, fiercer waves accumulating and exploding: a wave pounds on a balanced rock; the rock lurches with thunder-thud into the seething sea trough: another pounding thunder-roar, and the cliff quivers with tremor of walls in bombardment.

A lightning flash is stabbed into the sky and jabbed at by other flashes, their crazy neons jittering into word shapes, WHAT IS LOST NOW IS OUR HOME IN THIS WORLD. Immediate glimpse of monstrous vicious crocodile snouts thrusting out of the waves and flaming, fire-belching with deafening shattering booming reverberation and blinding eye-thunder (black and fire everywhere); could be warships, submarines, could be leviathans in their death-throes.

Now the cliff, in black-and-white flaps of fire and thunder, bashed and battered by waves and beaten to breaking-point; rocks, a whole buttress, loosen with earthquake rumble, start to slither; a whole segment of the cliff crumbles and falls away, bearing with it a tree, torn-up roots wildly writhing; the house hanging suspended, projecting over the now concave cliff verge, overhanging nothing.

Inside the bedroom, the sleeper has woken. In this dark room a stirring movement, the door opening, someone entering. Hands, frailly phosphorescent, extended, groping, delicately contacting the edges of furniture, feeling their way like blind hands. A blue ring flashes; two hands are joined, one leading the other, and flashing its bright ring; the hands moving through the dark house together, in darkness, out of the house; leaving it:

outside the tumult speeds up, the storm noise getting steadily madder; the flaming monsters vomiting more and more frenziedly, blasting each other;

finally wrecked and ruined and sinking, sizzling in sparks and white-hot seethe of lightning and steaming sea:

with deafening roar the entire cliff crumbles, collapses; the house curtseys, sinking forward slowly, turns over, slowly and gracefully disintegrates (walls fall outwards like sides of cardhouse), disappears.

The pandemonium is dimmed quickly into sound of rushing wind; dull, heavy and broken thumping of waves subsiding; then silence.

Two vague figures, one leading the other by the hand, seen receding far off under the quiet night sky where a few watery stars are starting to reappear.

A most remote, primordial scene. A large expanse of mountainous country, no trees, no water, no habitations. Although there are no really high peaks in sight one gets somehow the impression of being at a high altitude, on a plateau among the tops of the mountains. The rock formations are flattish, truncated, the higher tors assuming the shapes of miniature Table Mountains. The coloring a uniform cool lichen-grey.

The sun has just set and the sky is still faintly pink in the west behind a low blurring dust-haze; elsewhere it is a very limpid and unimpassioned shade of delicate lime-green. In the segment of sky opposite the sunset, above the crenellated horizon, a star, at first only just visible, growing momentarily brighter, assumes an elongated shape like a candle-flame. It is at first the only star to be seen: but very soon another, another, and then another, make their appearance. Towards this cross-shaped constellation, across the plateau in the fading light, a procession of vaguely feminine forms moves slowly on foot. The leader raises her hand in encouragement or in exhortation, points to the four stars. So swift is the passing of the subsequent flash that it is impossible to say whether ring or stars originated the light.

The pilgrimage continues to follow the stars which grow larger and brighter, more strangely shaped

until they reveal themselves as candle-flames in a small dark room with no windows or doors visible. The walls are scrawled over with dimly-seen symbols, pentacles, wands, swords, etc. There are shelves of books: a few phantom-glimmering shapes of vases or urns. B sits on the floor, reading by the light of the four candles set in their cross-shaped holder.

The Liaison Officer in his smart uniform is preparing to read out of his book again. There is the impression hanging about the dream that he has just finished a part of his lecture or sermon or whatever it is, and is about to start on something new. This he does, by reading in a clear cold voice which has perhaps grown somewhat more authoritarian in its inflexion.

Many people have said that retreats are undesirable and that they should be abolished because their existence constitutes a threat to the supremacy of the authorities whose powers ought to be absolute. But when a man says that he is going into retreat it does not mean he is evading the law, which is an impossibility anyhow: it means that he is effecting a change of authority, a transfer from one set of laws to another set at least equally mysterious and severe—so that he is certainly not making an escape of any sort. All that these retreats do is afford an alternative code, no less exacting and quite as incomprehensible as the one held in more general observance. But when it comes to the attitude of the authorities towards such institutions—here, I think, we are getting out of our depth.

In this connection it could be argued: if the authorities really are supreme, why should they permit the continued existence of a system which competes with their own? Is it not much more likely that the retreats are licensed by the authorities because, in some inscrutable way, they play their part in the established order?

There is even the possibility that the regime of the retreats, although it appears (superficially at least) totally different, is nothing but a disguised version of the regulations in force outside. This theory, improbable as it sounds, is supported by the fact that in certain contingencies the two spheres of authority indubitably converge, and perhaps even merge into one another if the critical nature of the emergency warrants it. But these eventualities are so rare and so little understood, the whole subject is so complicated by ambiguity and obscurity, that speculation is necessarily vague.

Actually, one is tempted to believe that the authorities are so perspicacious, so ingenious, that they have devised this method of tricking into conformity with the law people who might otherwise prove recalcitrant and badly adjusted. It is easy to see how a person of this type, thinking only of his own idiosyncrasies, would fall into the trap. He imagines that by going into retreat he will change his allegiance. And, indeed, once he is inside he becomes docile and content, believing that the old authorities control him no longer.

Meanwhile they, in a stronger position than ever, merely congratulate themselves on the success of their stratagem. The fact that their victory has been won in secret is immaterial; why should they, being all-powerful, wish to make an open display of their powers? All that they wanted has now been skilfully and pacifically achieved.

I hid my face in the lap of darkness like a lost child brought at last to his mother. Never again would I stray into the light: never again would I trust myself to a place where even those who sold their birthright for safety were not secure.

THE DREAMSCAPE languidly opens up. Conspectus of university town; early morning mist slowly clearing. The mist dispersal not mere evaporation but a sort of gradual unswathing, very gentle protracted tearing, rolling up and discarding, as of webs or excessively fragile tissue paper, disclosing buildings in careful succession. This process, though necessarily long-drawn out, progresses methodically with a certain businesslike efficiency. Enough should be seen of it to suggest the practiced unpacking and setting out of, say, a stock of valuable china.

View narrows to disclosure, from the ground upwards, of one particular tower. As mist wrappings are removed, there appears, on a carved ledge, a row of plump pigeons fast asleep with heads under their wings. Then, sighted up the shaft of the tower as if from its foot, the remote rococo summit, which in a second starts to revolve, discharges a musical-box carillon of tinkling notes which dance off, frisky white minims and semibreves, into the now blue sky. Back for a moment to the pigeons, untucking themselves, yawning, blinking, sleepily stretching their wings.

Now a switchover to an outlying residential street of the same town. Ahead, set back from the road in small flowerless lawn garden, a new white flat-roofed modern house, determinedly unembellished, simple rectangles superimposed like a construction of nursery building blocks. A path of concrete slabs leads to the front door which has a chromium ring, O-shaped, instead of a handle.

Inside, in one of the bedrooms upstairs, a child's cot. It is white, with bars at the sides; a brightly painted cock decorates the headboard, an owl the foot; the occupant lies motionless under puffed pale-blue eiderdown. Across the floor, which is covered in some hygienic greyish composition of cork or rubber, comes a tall brass-like woman of forty, her face somewhat like a photo of one of the hostesses seen in society papers; looking like and dressed like a hybrid nurse and socialite; her plucked eyebrows very arched, her lips painted bright red; costumed as if for a cocktail party; wearing a mackintosh apron tied round her waist.

In a series of brisk efficient motions she approaches the cot; lets down the side (with harsh buzz-saw rasp); bends stiff from the waist, her tightly sheathed hind parts glossy in taut satin; turns back the eiderdown. With her hard hands she reaches inside the woolly-white, lamb's-wool coverings (peeling them off as if they were part of a parcel or a cocoon) and grasps firmly, and after a moment lifts out a manikin, adeptly supported by her large hands under buttocks and shoulder-blades, dressed in grey-mottled and baggy tweeds: she sits on a chair; the manikin held on her knee and balancing there, limp dangling feet turned in like a ventriloquist's dummy. The woman zips open her diamanté-trimmed corsage; pulls out a long rubbery phallus-shaped nipple from the glans of which a few flakes of sawdust scale off; inserts this in the dummy's mouth in the style of a petrol feed.

Shot of the little pursed rosebud mouth under shaved upper lip busily sucking away (with lip-smacking and belching accompaniment). The pose held in gruesome travesty of madonna and child tableau. While this goes on the manikin visibly swelling, swelling, swelling, till at the end of the meal he is almost a full-sized man. The woman stands him on the floor while she tucks away the flaccid phallus-teat, zips up her dress, stands up.

Slight transitional pause. Next view is downwards from landing to hall (looking down steep-diving staircase), on the two foreshortened figures, the man's egg-head with incipient bald tonsure spot. The woman hustles him into professorial gown, jerks, tugs, pats, brushes him off; takes his hand, leads him out of the front door. Through this open door is seen a sliver of venomous green-raffia stage grass.

Chug-chug sound of a child playing at cars; high-pitched tooting horn; the woman reappears in the doorway, watching departure; her watchfulness holds for a few seconds. The woman turning, comes back inside; closing the door, the lock snicks shut; ripping loose apron-strings. The apron falls on the floor. Denting it with her high heels she walks over it to the wall-mirror, extracts a lipstick from gold-mesh bag, starts to repaint her mouth. In the mirror, close-up of her enormously enlarged brilliant moist raw red mouth, suggestive of fancified genital organ.

Now a complete change of scene. The professor has reached the college and is lecturing to his class. He stands on a dais behind a desk on which is a carafe of water and a tin trumpet. He is not quite tall enough for the height of the desk and so he stands on an old-fashioned church hassock with flaps at the ends. To his left, on the wall behind him, a large blackboard scrawled over with undecipherable words and symbols in colored chalks. (Conceivably some of these might be semi-intelligible words related to escapism; and one or two of the scribbles could be kindergarten obscenities, faces, figures.) On the right a phenomenally tall blank frosted-glass window reaches clear from floor to high domed ceiling. It holds its pair of stiff white fluted curtains rigidly to its sides in arms-downward-stretch position. Semicircular tiers of benches rising in front. The back of each bench forms a continuous curved shelf for the books of the row above. Only two tiers towards the center are occupied. (There could be a suggestion of upper and lower dentures in this.) The students are masks: upper row masculine, feminine lower. Except for the sex differentiation, which appears mainly in the arrangement and length of the painted hair, all are identical, characterless, with wide round eyes of respectful admiration, adulation, attention. The masks supported on spinal columns of spiral wire: similar wires representing arms terminated by limp chamois glove-hands half-stuffed with cotton. The hands are laid flat on the bookrests with books between; all are motionless.

The professor's voice continuous

wordless booming punctuated by an occasional NOW or YOU SEE. Sudden short tinny interjection of sound as he picks up toy trumpet and blows. Followed by immediate lifting and reaching out of curtain arms from the window, one arm to each row of students, arms gliding smoothly over the rows of limp glove-hands, touching off each hand in turn, retiring swiftly to the original attention posture at window. There is a faint twanging noise of quivering wires while the gloves are left gangling in palsied mimicry of jittery handwriting and the professor takes a long drink of water.

A resumption of the professorial booming (for a very short period this time), with attention gradually concentrating on the curtains, which appear holding themselves with watchdog vigilance at their window post. Climax comes with the curtains coiling, the curtain tentacles extending, delicately glissading along the mask rows, turning the masks to the blackboard (the professor chalks up O); masks spectrally twitching and trilling in twisted unison; the curtain arms coil high to the ceiling, weave there; then return to the window, to stiff and full arm's-length attention at each side of window, resume the same tense rigidity as before. As the wire vibration dies down, one after another, the masks topple, tumble, tip out of sight behind the benches. As the last one disappears the professor comes down from the hassock, from the dais, walks to the door of the lecture room.

Four seconds after he has gone out of the door the left curtain slowly draws itself across half the window. The right curtain slowly crosses to meet it.

A series of transient views tracks the professor's progress from lecture room to outer door of college. His black-moth-gown seen fluttering down long perspective of shadowed, tunnel-like stone corridor; emerging into high-groined and vaulted entrance hall, the grey stones of the floor with faint localized stippling of amethyst, topaz, ruby light spillings from stained-glass windows.

Numerous indistinct indications of other figures, gowned professors, student masks topping garments on coat-hangers, wires, hockey-sticks; all flickering spasmodically in different directions; all very indefinite, ephemeral.

Finally, a static black-and-white punctuation mark, a heavy dark ancient door under gothic arch. An old man's gnarled, unsteady, veined hand with border of frayed shirt-cuff, wear-shined and threadbare porter's sleeve, draws back bolts, turns key, loosens chain, with rusty rasping, jarring complaint of unoiled metal.

The door slowly opens.

First the pepper-and-salt trousers, then the whole of the professor, stepping out of the door, crossing empty and sunlit pavement in the cracks of which wild flowers, daisies, harebells, cowslips, primroses, are in bloom. A toy motor-car, painted red, stands at the curb. The professor packs and stuffs and forces himself into it; settles his feet on the pedals; squeezes a captious toot out of the rubber horn-bulb; vigorously pedals off. There is a squeaky noise from the chain driving the wire-spoked wheels. Short distance up street he signals with left arm stiffly extended;

turns left, disappears. The chain squeak briefly outlasts him.

Now the professor pedalling home through the quiet streets of the town; not a real-life town, of course. The sunshine is filtered through pink gauze. Colleges, churches, museums, etc., like birthday cakes in the gauzy light. Cuckoos fly out of belfries and cupolas as the clocks strike.

The professor keeps on pedalling, passes the entrance to a street which is in shadow. Glimpse down this street, emphasizing its shadowed contrast to the rest of the town. About two hundred yards along it, facing another way, a mass of full-sized people crowds silently outside a municipal building, a town hall or a police station, very dark-looking, very ominous, introducing an abrupt note of alarm. The professor does not look. He keeps on pedalling.

The sunlit street ribbons on unbroken down a gentle slope with the white play-block house at the end of it. The car, without free-wheel, running faster and faster downhill; the professor's knees pistoning faster and faster, almost grazing his chin.

Inside the house the woman who appeared earlier on is playing mah-jong with three visitors. These people are seen only in profile and are feminine, bloodless; with long proboscis noses, like Javanese silhouettes stamped out of metal, very frigidly and ophidianly malignant. The mah-jong tiles forming the walls behind which they are sitting are covered with money symbols, deeds, bonds, coins of various currencies; power symbols, scepters, whips, bribes, skins; diapers, feeding bottles; phallic signs.

Rapid survey of this somewhat provincial pretentious drawing-room of a would-be-modern intellectual. Smooth, pale, faintly glazed planes of walls, built-in furniture, unstained woods: squarish, low, upholstered couch; easy chairs covered in zebra-stripe fabric: the emasculate fireplace, without mantelpiece, without fire, meekly impounded by chaste light wood bands: wall alcoves, interiorly tinted, and displaying such objects as negro carvings and/or very consciously quaint period pieces, china dogs, red and blue glinting lusters, wax flowers under fragile cloches. Bookshelves with volumes of philosophy, psychology by the more superficial writers, books issued by "advanced" publishers, a few up-to-the-moment novels, poems, pamphlets, "advanced" publications generally, a few literary quarterlies and art papers. There would be not more than two or three not-very-original paintings in pale frames on the walls: still life of the slick Slade student apple-and-wine-glass variety, or etiolated impressionist water-color, or possibly pastel-smudged portrait or overloaded oil landscape in crude colour discords. There would probably be an absence of flowers in the room; or perhaps a single white pottery jar of tall grasses or shell flowers.

This room the professor enters in his black gown; with light short tripping steps advances across the neutral carpet; pirouettes; simpers and postures. He stands holding the pose, feet in the fifth position, skirts of his gown extended to fullest width and held between thumbs and forefingers, both little fingers curled and archly pointing.

In their alcoves the dangling glass lobes of the

lusters begin to swing and oscillate gently, set up a faint tinkling applause.

Now a quick circling view of the whole rather phony prosperous enclosed room dithering faintly appreciative: into this circle, very complacent, the professor relaxes coyly from his pose: acknowledging the slight rustle of handclapping from the mah-jong players he sits down in the exact center of the couch.

The players rise from the table, group themselves round him. The visitors (always in profile) take positions on each side of him on the couch, the third sits on the floor at his feet. From attitudes of admiration their flat snake eyes are upon him in bitter malice, contempt or envy. His own woman is standing behind him, her face tiger-possessive, triumphant; she sets her fingers proprietorially on his head, absently twists his thin hair into kewpie tuft.

This tableau abruptly shattered by sudden rude surge of clamoring, knocking, at outer door of the house. With utmost possible effect of shock, enormous figures, in dark uniforms, bursting into the room, crowding in one after the other, surrounding the couch, brandishing, with threatening gestures, some document (Demand? Indictment?) under the professor's nose.

He jumps up, astounded and outraged, thrusting the three visitors aside in rising (they collapse stiffly with metallic jingle and disappear); the woman behind the sofa gestures imperiously; calls out an unidentifiable order: she is at once submerged by the uniforms; seen struggling for a moment; disappears.

The professor is ringed, pressed on all sides by the massed uniforms, fear now coming out on his face like sweat. He glances round quickly, his face more and more afraid. He clutches his gown, pulls it higher and higher up round his shoulders, hunches his neck in it, muffles his head in its folds; and out of this hiding-place yells shrilly some protest or appeal, indignation in the start of the sounds, panic towards the end.

Two huge uniformed arms are extended from each side simultaneously.

They take hold of the gown, twitch at it derisively, contemptuously snatch it away.

The manikin cowers on the floor, grovels between them, his head with bald spot lolling limp on dummy stalk-neck to the floor.

As the arms grapple him every ornament in the room sets up a thin mad screeching.

A china dog leaps frantically from its shelf and dives under the couch with reversed curlicue tail between its legs.

A glass goblet falls; heavy boots tramp it to dust.

The boots and the forest of dark legs close in, amalgamate into black blob-blot. The blob bulges, spreads steadfastly up to and over everything; blots out the room with a bulging and bursting of black bubble, inky cuttlefish ejaculation; and the brittle death trills still bleating. Blotchout.

LONG ago I had embraced the night and given myself to darkness. The gentle whispers of rain had consoled me; kind quiet shadows had been my friends.

Why was I led astray by a tiger brightness? Why did a false sun lure me so far from home?

True, I had not actually surrendered to daylight. But I had looked too long into dazzling and sunbright faces and stayed too long within the gates of day. My eyes had looked at something forbidden, and seen what they should never have seen, and now sight itself had gone out of them.

Now from the dark and solitary place where I belonged I would not stir again. When voices called to me I refused to answer. I stopped my ears with the black robe of night and pulled the folds of darkness about my head. Never again would I see the blinding glare of enemy eyes or hear the thudding of disastrous feet.

IS IT or is it not the Liaison Officer who sits at a desk in the middle of this dream? The face looks the same and so does the little neat beard—can it be turning grey?—but why is he wearing an elegant dark suit instead of a uniform? Perhaps not his almost too elegant clothes, but his surroundings, including the big glossy desk where he sits writing, suggest the prosperous professional man, without precisely indicating which profession. On the whole, the room looks more like a doctor's consulting-room than anything else; and yet that doesn't seem quite the right label. The divan and the massive, costly, dead-looking furniture could belong to any successful practitioner. But there are some rather queer mystical pictures and ornaments which don't seem to fit in. Is it a crucifix or a primitive negro priapus hanging there on the wall? It's hard to make anything out in the dim light. A row of books under the desk-lamp can be distinguished as medical textbooks mixed up with books on magic, mythology, philosophy, metaphysics, religion.

The man sitting behind the books has finished his writing. He screws the cap on to his fountain-pen, looks up, and as he moves the gold lettering gleams on the epaulets which he is now seen to be wearing with the insignia of his rank. He leans back comfortably in his chair, gathering together the written sheets, which he holds in one hand (keeping the other free for an occasional restrained gesture) while he reads aloud from them in the smooth nicely-modulated voice of a trained actor.

Who are the authorities and where are they to be found? Do they operate from one central focus or from various scattered bureaus with, possibly, a main headquarters in supreme control of the whole organization? These are questions which everyone asks but to which no satisfactory replies are forthcoming. Admittedly, there are so-called initiates who claim to possess information, and one has heard of people whose minds have been set at rest by these individuals. And yet if you or I decide to go into the matter for ourselves our investigations never seem to lead anywhere. Supposing that certain persons have, as they assert, obtained enlightenment from some unknown source, it would seem that they are unable, or perhaps not allowed, to illuminate others, except in rare and selected instances. What happens when you approach such a person with a genuine wish for communication? He will most likely start off by talking to you in a straightforward easy way that at once gives a favorable impression of frankness. Make yourself at home, my friend, he says, by implication if not in so many words. Relax, and listen while I explain everything to you in simple language.

This ingenious technique is, in fact, so convincing that anyone may well be taken in by it, lulled into an uncritical state of mind merely by the soothing quality of manner and words. Quite probably it is not until one has been ushered out of the warm room and is walking home through the frosty air that one really begins to reflect on the interview in an objective way, and to realize that one is absolutely no wiser than before.

At this stage I imagine the average inquirer is apt to abandon the whole affair, considering that he has made an effort adequate to preserve his integrity. Besides, he may think, matters so deep and so hard to approach are certainly dangerous and forbidden and I had better not dabble in them or I shall get into trouble.

On the other hand, someone of greater tenacity and tougher moral fiber may decide to return to the charge. I won't be fobbed off like this, he says to himself: and before his next visit he carefully thinks out and memorizes a series of leading questions. But no matter how cool-headed he is or how well he has studied and framed his questions, the result is precisely the same as before. This time, to be sure, the technique will be somewhat different. Instead of the misleading simplicity of the previous occasion, the interrogator now encounters a complexity of specious rhetoric which is woven before him like those unbelievably fine Chinese embroideries which seem to be without beginning or end. The visitor doesn't forget a single question; he puts forward every point in due order. And to every question and point he receives not only an answer but an elaborate homily, a whole lengthy peroration full of learned allusions which a layman would hardly be likely to follow.

But the questioner is a man of superior intelligence, and determination as well. He sticks to his guns, he forces his brain to keep pace with all that is being said.

And now a curious and disheartening phenomenon makes its appearance; a phenomenon of which there appears to be no explanation. It seems to him that each separate sentence is comprehensible. He is convinced that he understands everything. And, in fact, the various themes, taken one by one, do give an effect of being quite lucid and reasonable, and he hurries home to get the whole thing down on paper while it is fresh in his mind.

Yet no sooner does he begin to concentrate on the subject *as a whole* than he is overcome by a paralyzing mental confusion. The explanations, the allusions, the arguments which individually seemed clear enough, inexplicably lose their significance when viewed as component parts of a pattern, and dissolve into empty verbosity. Hour after hour the unfortunate inquirer sits motionless with his brain in a turmoil, his pen in his hand, unable to write down a single word. Disregarding the voices of his family or his friends, not noticing when it is time to eat or to go to bed, he ponders endlessly over what he has heard, forcing concentration to its *n*th power in a desperate endeavor to track and pin down the meaning which he once thought was within his grasp, but which has now tantalizingly and mysteriously concealed itself in an intricate maze of incomprehensible phraseology. So it goes on, his thoughts racing fruitlessly and interminably, until sheer mental exhaustion compels him to give in.

Ah, how well one knows the whole horrid cycle, from confidence to uncertainty, to bewilderment, and finally to utter chaos and despair. What is the key to it all? What attitude should one take up? The fact is, and I suppose we must accept it, that for the great majority it is impossible to find out anything about the authorities. But to resign oneself to ignorance is indeed hard. Everyone knows that the authorities exercise supreme control over each one of us, even down to the most trivial details of our lives: and this is even specifically stated in the writings of our ancient teachers. Human beings can hardly be expected to refrain from trying to throw a little light on such vital mysteries: particularly as some unconscious impulse deep in our natures seems to be continually turning our thoughts in that direction.

Who has not, when walking in an unfamiliar part of the town, felt one of those sudden queer psychological shocks which dart like arrows, like premonitions, out of the blue? One may be hurrying along thinking about some personal matter or about an important appointment ahead. All at once, quite without rhyme or reason, the thread of thought snaps, one looks up and sees a big dingy building on the other side of the street, a warehouse possibly, or an old-fashioned office block, which seems to be empty because the shutters are all closed and scraps of paper and leaves have blown on to the dusty doorstep. It's the sort of unattractive unremarkable place you might pass a hundred times without noticing; but today it catches your eye just as an importunate beggar might catch hold of your sleeve. After all it isn't deserted, because between the slats of the shutters dim lights are gleaming. And suddenly the idea comes into your head that perhaps now, at this very moment while you are passing by, in one of the rooms behind those drab shutters, at a worm-eaten desk, among bundles of papers tied up with red or green tape, with scratchy old-fashioned pen-strokes, your fate is being inscribed.

Or something like this may happen while you are out for a walk in the country: you feel yourself quite alone, for an hour you haven't seen one living creature, not even a dog or a horse in a field, you seem to be miles from anywhere. And then in this solitude, out of the bushes at the side of the road, a sly face looks out at you, the face of an old man with a beard and a big hat such as is seldom worn these days. Just for a second he looks out at you. It's really surprising to meet anyone in such a lonely place; but instead of saying Good day, he draws back, disappears into the wood, and you don't see him again. What is it makes you feel that this old man has been watching you, perhaps following you for some time, hidden among the trees: that he has perhaps been sent to that out-of-the-way spot on purpose to see and report afterwards which track you are following, whether you turn to the right or the left at the cross-roads at the foot of the hill?

Nobody knows the exact significance of these feelings which all of us have experienced: but that they bear some relation to our close surveillance by the authorities appears certain. If only it were possible to find out something definite. One feels under constant observation. One has the conviction that every trifling act is noted and set down either against one or in one's favour. And at the same time one hasn't the faintest clue to the standards by which one is being judged. How is it possible to avoid anxiety and indecision when a move of any kind involves the whole of one's future status?

Well, it's no good trying to take matters into our own hands; nor is it much good consulting anyone else. All we can do is walk circumspectly and hope for the best; always remembering that whole trains of unimaginable events may follow some incident which seems quite trivial to us, such as, for example, the act of telephoning instead of writing a letter to someone we know.

When everything's said and done, unfortunately, we find ourselves in the position of children whose parents have gone to the theatre, leaving them alone in the dark house. Yes, we are forced, if we are honest, to make the saddest of all admissions when it comes to the last resort: Alas, we do not understand these things.

What ages it took us to get to the end of our journey. At times it seemed as if we never should arrive anywhere, but spend our whole lives travelling. The natives of the countries we passed through must have thought us a funny lot, all of us wearing the same face (though our sizes were different, and our clothes too, of course). Some of us would have liked to settle down in one of these countries, some in another. And I think we all occasionally wished in our secret hearts that we'd never embarked on the expedition. But we couldn't go back once we had started. There was nothing for it but to keep moving on, even if we didn't know where we were going. It wasn't a pleasure trip at any stage; but sometimes the going was terribly hard and slow and exhausting; those were the times when we tried to keep up our spirits by singing. We don't know where we're going, we sang then, but we're on our way. We got discouraged though, all the same, however loudly we sang.

Besides the hardships of the journey itself, there was the isolation and the uncertainty about what we should find at the end of it, supposing we ever did get to our destination. It was impossible not to feel anxious from time to time, and homesick, as well. How could we help remembering the place where we'd lived long ago, where people were kind and smiling? How could we help reflecting that the smiles and the kindness would have been still there for us to enjoy if we hadn't been so independent? We used to think of that place always flooded with summer sunshine, while we were travelling far away in stony forgotten regions under a winter sky.

It was winter when we arrived at a place which we thought at first was the right one. The inhabitants came out to meet us and took us in: they took our arms and took us inside walls, and then we saw that the windows were barred and that the doors could not be opened. We became frightened, smelling the caged smell that was in the place, and seeing the locked garden where men with dead eyes swept the unfallen leaves. We saw sleepers laid out in a mass-grave, and officials going amongst them with sleep in their hands. We were more frightened then, we looked at one another and whispered, What kind of sleep is this? knowing now that certainly we had not reached the right destination.

From there we escaped finally, and travelled farther, and in the end we arrived, in spite of all the obstacles. How glad we were to think we had got to our own place! How glad we were to be able to rest at last! Yes, it seems wonderful that the dangers are all behind us. But even now we sometimes wonder about things, and think of the lost sun and the smiles that we knew in the beginning. We suffered much in avoiding those treacherous smiles: we passed through many trials to escape that traitorous sun.

Now we are safe at last. We are secure. We are at peace. But even in the midst of the security and the peace . . . Still, at certain moments . . . we wonder, secretly, if it was worth it . . . if peace and security are really worth the splendour they cost to buy.

It is night; and there is nothing false here. Night is reliable. Night does not dazzle us with treacherous fires. Night keeps a dark enduring silence for us . . . like sleep, deep sleep. By our own will we came here and tasted sleep before there was any need, because we loved to gaze at the face of night. But not quite at home . . . even among loved shadows . . . we can't forget altogether the splendid sun . . . we sometimes have to dream of the place we came from.

The blissful eye, conscientiously keeping an eye on everything in its turn, takes a turn at eyeing microbic matters, applies itself to the eyepiece (microscope by Negretti and Zambra), and makes a leisurely tour of the slide-wide situation.

A peaceful pastoral scene is here displayed on the fluorescent field, quite in order and as it should be, unexciting, of course, but who is not prepared to sacrifice whatsit to whatsit these days? There is, we think, general agreement that we all have to face a period of whatsit and lessened whatsit for some time to come.

In addition to those of us who are actively engaged in one of the whatsits, very many other people are turning towards whatsit as an outlet for their thoughts and energies, and either as a means of increasing whatsit for whatsit motives, or as a whatsit to take the place of other whatsits not now within their reach.

There is no more gratifying sight for the enthusiast than a contented culture of healthy whatsits placidly browsing upon the pabulum scientifically prepared by those who have studied whatsits and understand the many problems which may cause anxiety.

What is it that emerges from this droplet of broth, or is it bouillon, deposited with professional precision upon the slide? What menacing creatures are these, battened on the nourishing fluid, which now encircle and stalk down their unconscious victims?

The successful preservation of whatsit often depends on the ability of the whatsit to combat and destroy the various whatsit and whatsit whatsits, which maneuver so much more rapidly, and which, if not speedily checked, will often ruin the whole of a whatsit in a whatsit. The great secret is to be continually on the watch, and to attack the whatsit at the outset before it has had time to gain a whatsit.

On this occasion the experimenter (though doubtless familiar with every branch of the technique), perhaps in the pursuit of further knowledge, makes no attempt to interfere with the fate of these hapless humble martyrs to science, but dispassionately observes the onslaught of the voracious attackers who tear into their prey like tigers and devour them wholly till no single trace remains.

But Nemesis is not far away.

No whatsit need remain in any uncertainty about the kind of whatsit to use in a whatsit, for information is freely available to all and it is the duty of every whatsit one of us to make himself familiar with a few simple whatsits for whatsit. Remember that a whatsit's whatsit may depend on your whatsit. Whatsit now

Swift indeed is the retribution which overtakes the aggressors; and for a display of poetic justice it would be hard to rival the terrible scene which now ensues. A third infinitesimal drop is planted deftly on the slide, an agent so powerful that, extending rapidly in a thin film around and over the fierce corpuscular conquerors, it instantaneously absorbs them into itself, eliminating them in a second by a horrid process of ingurgitation.

Tiring, one imagines, of this close concentration upon bacillic dramatics, a simple adjustment on the part of the eye (Pinto et Issaverdens precision instruments) scales the operational field up to major proportions. A truly astounding scene is forthwith presented, one guaranteed to strike the stoutest heart with terror and amazement. The very seat of reason itself quakes under the visual impact of this awful spectacle, hardly to be expressed in ordinary words. How can one describe even the background, that dark and whirling storm of fiery particles, blinding and burning and asphyxiating at the same time? It's a fog and yet it's a fire, intolerable heat combined with suffocating obscurity. Through this murky inferno, huge armor-plated monsters, blind and mad, are charging in all directions, demented, hideous, driven by their Gadarene frenzy to charge each other in indiscriminate fury, stampeded and possessed by maniacal fiends.

Even the perennially untroubled eye of the Heaven-Born prefers not to linger on this unspeakable shambles

and passes on through the world wilderness of death to a large remote semi-demolished, sham-antique building. Under powerful moonshine lamp-flood black forms are busily hauling and hoisting and heaving apart various beams, arches, windows, etc., of this fake medieval edifice. View of the partially dismantled whole narrows down to a doorway; moves over trampled ground to a mock mulberry tree which two sweaty workmen in singlets are preparing to remove. They unhook several large boughs hinged to the main trunk, drop them carelessly on the ground (the torn faded fabric leaves flutter dusty in dust); wrench remainder of tree from its socket; struggle off, lugging it between them.

The general view again, very briefly, indefinitely, outlines blurred and figures eliminated; retreating almost immediately to distant glimpse of roughly similarly-shaped sand-castle on a deserted beach in moonlight. The tide comes in quickly. Views of successive small summer waves breaking (with soft soooooon sound), opening white-lipped mouths on the sand, each sucking a few inches nearer the castle.

The first wave reaches the castle wall. The white wavelips suck at the sand with their sibilance, insidiously: soooon soooooon sooooon (each wave sucking a little harder, higher, undermining the castle).

The sand walls spread, subside, sink, settle, submerge—their soft almost soundless sigh sunk in the sea sound.

In a house where furnished seaside lodgings are rented a girl, asleep in her bed, green slippers under the bed as she kicked them off toe-to-heel, dreams, stirs and hears the subsidence (it is only a dressing-gown slipping off the end of the bed); she does not wake; although she changes position.

The empty beach with the sand now covered by water, smooth and full. The moon gravely passes with quiet deliberation behind a cloud, drawing after her all detail; leaving only the tranquilly breathing breast of dark and murmurous water; which the eye observes, as it seems, pensively, and one is anthropomorphically inclined to believe, with relief in respite, until

goddess no longer of the moody crested tire,

quick-change artist and record-holder, out steps the twenty-one-year-old lieutenant-colonel—the youngest in the whatsit army—wearing steel helmet, rakishly askew, eccentric battledress copiously stippled with pig's blood, bedroom slippers with soft woollen pompons (I intend to invade whatsit in comfort); his face is blacked like a nigger minstrel's with white eye-circles, one emitting searchlight illumination: through the second orifice a whizzing stream of machine-gun bullets, exploding bombs, rockets, clods of earth, power-diving planes, bombers, fighters, vampires, anopheles-size and vicious, in inexhaustible swarms.

The searchlight beam points erratically hither and thither, in the manner of a retriever questing for game, over the vast slow-seething seabulk which is now apperceptible as a sort of time symbol holding locked in its dark plasma the innumerable bubbles of all past and future eventualities.

At irregular intervals the beam oscillates violently in the agitation of finding, then slowly fixes, freezing in its terminal circle small distant sharp scenes of topical interest. As,

an idealized country house in sunny summery landscape, roses round the door, elm-muffled peaceable strokes of church clock striking the tea hour, strawberries and cream and deck-chairs on the lawn, unseen pigeons cooing, every exile's sentimental picture of home.

Twilight gathers quickly; a bleak wind rising overturns the deserted chairs: the roses droop, wither, fall, their petals are blown away; the pigeon-coos hoarsen to ominous hooting as a huge spectral white owl with lambent eyes sweeps stealthily past, concentrating to pounce as it disappears; immediately afterwards a thin mouse death-shriek is heard.

In deepening darkness dimly seen conspiratorial forms, wearing some kind of horrific disguise-uniform (Inquisition or Ku-Klux-Klan suggestion) by unclear and rapid manipulation convert the house to traditional haunted-house aspect.

The Hanged Man swings from a black tree; he is looking at something unseen in the air; spinning slowly in the wind with desolate bone creaking; muttering, I am too old to be in a tree. A mongrel pup, starved ribcage on four matchsticks, slinks in and out of sight. Mist wraiths coagulate, hover lugubriously, disintegrate, among dark shapes of bushes or tombstones or crouching things. After slight pause, a small white bone falls like a full stop on the black grass.

Now inside the house: a storm lantern flickers feebly on dusty and empty rooms that the wind whimpers through, and on the uneasy group of neophytes herded together. These are boys of about fourteen, with dumb-bucolic or vicious-urban-degenerate faces sniggering in discomfort, and with restless movements and whispers hiding their half-alarm. They are dressed in badly fitting uniforms of cheap coarse material, some with jackets sagging loose to the knees, some with tight sleeves which fail to cover their wrists. They are armed with weapons contrastingly expensive, efficient, ultra-modern and deadly looking. Carrying out their orders, they move through the rooms, a few displaying exaggerated toughness, the others alternatively scared and vacuously amused by the various trick manifestations, hidden traps, skulls springing out of cupboards, chains clanking, lights suddenly flashing, doors suddenly opening or slamming, moans, screams, howls, etc.

Finally the roof lifts up like a lid and the lieutenant-colonel is seen hovering batlike and spraying from the poison ducts at the back of his vampire fangs a fine rain of blood with which the upturned faces are thinly spattered. Simultaneously his voice, very much amplified, yells through the loudspeaker, On your toes, boys. Remember whatsit. There's a whatsit. Kill the swine. Kick his guts out.

As his image slowly fades it develops a recognizable though incomplete resemblance to the Liaison Officer. At the instant of disappearance the rim of his steel helmet catches the light and hangs in mid-air, a halo-like, phosphorescent ellipse which evaporates as the loudspeaker switches to soundtrack of war horror film

linking up with

a cinema audience in tightly-packed hall. The rows of people seen from the back all exactly similar somewhat elongated heads with protuberant ears. A big flag with crossed emblem hangs over the screen where an air-raid is shown in progress. Deafening accompaniment of appropriate noises: bombs, rockets, ack-ack, sirens, shouts, clanging bells of fire engines, ambulances, etc. Walls seen crumbling, A.R.P. and N.F.S. personnel search through wreckage and rubble for victims under mobile arc-lamps.

A woman is carried by on a stretcher; where her face was, foot-long splinters of glass project like porcupine quills. A growl of rage, baited-animal sound, travels along the watching rows of the audience.

Quick over the road to the movie theatre on the other side. The rows of people here seen from the back all exactly similar somewhat square heads with protuberant ears. A big flag with circular emblem hangs over the screen where an air-raid is shown in progress. Deafening accompaniment of appropriate noises: bombs, rockets, ack-ack, sirens, shouts, clanging bells of fire engines, ambulances, etc. Walls seen crumbling, A.R.P. and N.F.S. personnel hunt through wreckage and rubble for victims under mobile arc-lamps. A woman is carried by on a stretcher; where her face was, foot-long splinters of glass project like porcupine quills. A growl of rage, baited-animal sound, travels along the watching rows of the audience.

Quickly the audiences of the two theatres crowding blackly out, overflowing the street like opposing ant-swarms. A rumbling roar goes up as they converge upon one another, interpenetrate.

The searchlight beam (now for the sake of convenience to be identified with the untroubled eye up above) wanders restlessly:

after a not arbitrary number of glimpses of world happenings,

roams towards a huge solitary fang-shaped rock, almost a mountain, jutting sheer out of the ocean, sleek oil-black faintly polished, belted with white scalloped beading of foam. A sudden long inexplicable swell gathers on the smooth water, mounting quickly to tidal-wave size, travels increasingly rapidly and toweringly to the rock; at the moment of impact the eyebeam telescopes into close-up of the shattering wave with heavy spray mane wind-combed and white from the black wave blown back.

In still closer analysis, the spray particles brightly illuminated, particularized, individualized, metamorphosed into papers of all descriptions.

Envelopes (with stamps of various countries, airmail stamps, Opened by Censor, D.D.A. stickers, O.H.M.S. signs, etc.) addressed in various handwritings or typewritten to places all over the world. Letters from lovers, banks, businesses, ministries, consulates, etc.; on embossed paper, thin paper, papers with printed headings, pages torn from exercise books. Birth, marriage, death certificates; diplomas, passports, dossiers, warrants, licences, ballot cards, invitations, tickets, checks, coupons, leaflets, cables, menus, currency notes, programs, manuscripts, drawings, photographs, labels, press-cuttings. These appear briefly (there is barely time to read them) with headlines in utter confusion. As

Gas leads suicide methods this winter. Shaw mumbles no in beard to love notes. Mayan temple hieroglyphics used as play-suit trimmings. No bass violinists in Folsom Prison. Atom Bomb opens new era in world destruction, entire city vaporized in black rain, victims vanish. Bishop thanks God for science.

There are perhaps one or two full paragraphs

Phosgene is the most practical and economical gas

for the production of quick death. While mustard-gas casualties are a long time in hospital, sometimes several months, there is nothing about them, immediately after being gassed, to inspire terror in other troops. With phosgene, however, if heavily gassed, men will be dropping dead like flies in a few hours. . . .

The impact of his body loosened the jam and started the coal moving downward to the funnel in the center of the floor. While his companions ran for aid, Seery flailed about and when police of Emergency Squad 4 reached the scene only his head and shoulders were visible. The bottom of an ashcan was ripped out and lowered to him as an improvised caisson. A rope was then dropped and planks were laid on top of the moving coal on which Fire Captain Charles Kuchas of Hook and Ladder Co. 24 clambered to Seery and administered a hypodermic. Then the Rev. W. J. Faricker of the Church of the Epiphany made the same dangerous journey to administer the last rites of the Catholic Church. As Father Faricker finished the rope snapped and Seery was sucked beneath the surface. . . .

Take a pleasant breezy jaunt with Jimmy Fidler, on location every day at the Mirror. . . .

Finally the whole mass of papers flying, whirling through the air like Alice's pack of cards. The paper storm condenses, recedes, spirals into funnel-shaped white cloud-whirl, tornado, travelling away at great speed over perfectly featureless, blank, near-black field: vanishing. The neutral shadowblank holds for a moment of discharging tension as the blissful eyes up above defocus slowly.

I can't remember the journey or who arranged it. No one told me where I was going. No one told me the name of the shadow house or why I was brought there.

Some things about the place were confusing. There were wet nights when it seemed to be the house where my mother lived. Sometimes when the rain struck at the window I called my mother's face to the black glass in the way a fisherman draws a fish to the surface of the water. Then it was hard to tell which face was my own.

Sometimes the shadow house was extremely quiet: vigilant silence crouched against every door. Sometimes the walls rang with tremendous music, Israfel sang, whose heart-strings are a lute, and all the ghosts of China twittered like crazy birds.

Sometimes my mother's familiars, sadness and boredom, loitered among the shadows: then I looked out of the window quickly.

My window was a magic glass which gave everything it reflected a kind face. Even hostility and chaos smiled in that mirror. When I looked out of the window everything became friendly and clear and simple. All day I could watch the white sky children wreathing light-hearted dances in their playground, while the air cherished them like a mother. And in the night my own mother came to the window to meet me, strange, solitary; splendid with countless stars; my mother Night; mine, lovely, mine. My home.

IT'S RATHER dark in the house where B has gone, and this isn't because it's evening outside. Of course, sometimes it is night out of doors, and then you'd expect the house to be dark indeed: but curiously enough there's very little difference inside between the night and the day. It's always twilight in those rooms where a lamp or a candle is just as likely to be burning at noon as in the small hours of the morning.

The house is really difficult to describe. You can say that it's in a town, in a long street of other houses. But that only conveys the vaguest impression, if it isn't actually misleading, for some of the upstairs windows look clean into the country with its lakes and streams and fields and forests and villages and the majestic mountains behind. It's no easier to give a picture of the interior either. Like most old places, this house has been altered and enlarged again and again so that the rooms are of all shapes and sizes and periods, opening one into another, or linked by galleries or flights of steps leading up and down in the most unexpected and unconventional way. One circular tower room, for instance, appears to have been built on quite haphazard, as if the architect had overlooked the necessity for connecting it with the rest of the building, and had only added as an afterthought a crooked little staircase hidden away in a corner which you might pass a dozen times without noticing. This irregularity of design makes it hard to find your way about in the house. It's such a rambling old place, there are so many rooms, and all of them half-dark, that you can never be absolutely certain you've been into every one.

B herself is often surprised when she is wandering in the passages to find that she has come to a door which she has never seen before. And this is particularly apt to happen just when she feels that she has at last mastered the plan of the different floors.

It almost seems as if alterations were continually taking place in the outlying parts of the house, certain rooms changing their shape or position or even disappearing entirely, and other new rooms proliferating in distant corridors: while the main part of the construction, the hall, kitchens, dining-room, library, principal bedrooms and so on, remain more or less stabilized. Certainly, minor changes are liable to occur even in these rooms; but they are unimportant and chiefly confined to differences of furniture, decoration or general arrangement. Thus, in place of a window, there may one day appear some ancient half-indistinguishable portrait of a state dignitary in solemn robes. And then very possibly within a few hours a window will again have taken the picture's place: but this time the window, instead of overlooking the street as before, will be facing on to a formal paved yard, bounded by high walls, and with a clipped shrub growing in each corner.

On the face of it, this looks like a lot of unnecessary expenditure of energy. It's hard to conceive any acceptable explanation of such changeability; unless the proprietors have adopted some complicated eclectic system with regard to the place. The best way, as in all these obscure matters, is simply to accept the situation without inquiring into causality, which would most likely be incomprehensible even if brought to light.

B, in any event, does not speculate about what goes on. These constant unpredictable variations, which some people might find disconcerting, to her constitute one of the great charms of the house. The pleasant anticipation of novelty turns the opening of every door into an adventure.

How does a girl like B feel, you may wonder, alone in this great dark place? The question can be answered in four simple words: B is at home. And she's not lonely either. Her companions are the many mirrors which hang all over the house in the various rooms. Probably there has never been a house which contained as many mirrors as this one. Mirrors framed in every imaginable style, from the huge glass in the salon with its magnificent eagle whose wide wings, glimmering with dim gilt in the dusk, seemed poised already in imperial flight, to the convex circle, no larger than a plate, which microcosmically reflects in steely recession the window at the turn of the stairs and a whole pinpoint Breughel landscape beyond. Long cheval glasses lean inquiringly in the bedrooms like strangers wishing to ask the way. In alcoves, in the passages, on landings, you will unexpectedly catch, just as you sometimes catch someone else's eye in a crowd, the subdued and watchful gleam of a mirror. And in every one of these mirrors B recognizes the fair-haired girl who is her closest friend.

Even without this mirror friend there would be plenty of entertainment to be had just by looking out of the windows. Sometimes, on certain days or in certain rooms, the curtains are drawn, and then of course it's inadvisable to attempt to look outside. But usually there is nothing to prevent you from studying the view. What a variety of views there are too. That's what makes window-gazing from this house so delightful.

Perhaps it's Christmas-time in the street. You can sit on the wide window-seat sheltered by a wine-colored velvet curtain and watch the snow feathers falling. The children are throwing snowballs as they run home in the twilight, their cheeks are bright red, they wear ear-muffs and warm mittens and little round caps made of fur. Their movements are like a dance. What a joy it is to watch such spontaneous happiness.

The tongues of the bells in the church steeple at the end of the street dart sharp and clean as icicles in the freezing air. The sky is the deep blue of sapphires, the snow burns blue-white, lighted windows blossom one after the other.

In the house opposite they are having a party. A huge holly wreath tied with red satin ribbon hangs on the door knocker. Gold light streams from the windows, and inside you can see the gorgeous Christmas-tree and the guests in their fine clothes. In one room people are dancing to the music of a piano and violin: in another, boys and girls are just sitting down to a table decorated with flowers and candles and toys. How gay all the faces are! What peace and friendliness inside the festive rooms; and the beautiful frozen night out of doors. It makes you feel warm and comfortable just to look at it all.

Or, maybe, delicate muslin ruffles are floating gently in and out of the open window in a warm breeze. The air enters scented with roses, with honeysuckle and clover, fresh with the smell of grass which men have been cutting all day long in the fields. Stripped to the waist, their torsos beautiful as light bronze, the strong young haymakers rhythmically swing their scythes through the final swaths. The heavy haywains lumber home in the dusk. From the village rises the sound of singing and laughter; a cheerful clatter of pans comes from the kitchens where women in bright aprons are preparing the evening meal. Lovers walk in the orchards under the ripening fruit. Grave and benign like archangels, the white winged mountains stand in the darkening sky.

Yes, there's always something fascinating to be seen from the windows. And then there's the house itself, a perpetual source of interest and surprise. Why, you could easily spend a lifetime investigating the library alone. Not to mention the pictures, the clocks, the tapestries, and the curious objects stored in the different rooms; the attics crowded with trunks, every one packed full of unimaginable and exciting treasures; the porcelain, silver, silk, crystal, ivory, jade, collected through many centuries and in many lands; the clothes folded away in the cupboards; the very pots and pans in the kitchen, the canisters full of strange spices, the herbs and cordials and preserves, the vast stone urnlike crocks on the storeroom floor.

It's really impossible to mention even a fraction of the riches contained in a house so inexhaustibly endowed with wonders from all over the world, as well as with its own unique, complex, incomparable individuality. You get confused when you try to describe it; the mind is embarrassed by such a wealth of material; you hardly know where to begin or where to leave off.

Well, the line has to be drawn somewhere: and that's why it seems useless to say any more except that no discriminating person would ever willingly leave such a house once they had taken up residence in it; or find any other house even tolerable afterwards.